THE
CAROUSEL SHOPPE
& OTHER STORIES

CHUCK CULVER

THUMBPRINT
PRESS

Library of Congress Catalog Card Number: 96-61451
ISBN 0-9654951-0-8 Cloth
ISBN 0-9654951-1-6 Paper

Published by THUMBPRINT PRESS, through
a grant from the Charles A. Masters Foundation

Cover Design and Illustration: Carol Kappel

Thumbprint Press
283 Butterfield Road
San Anselmo, CA 94960

Printed in the United States of America

To my children.

contents

a c k n o w l e d g m e n t s

These stories first appeared in the following publications:

"A Season For Storms" in *Gulf Coast:
A Journal Of Literature & Fine Arts*

"Whatever Happened To Grossfield?" in *Grab-A-Nickel*

"Ancient Lives," "Instincts," "Marcie's Visit, and
"Duty's The Boat To Gull Island" in *Bust Out Stories*

"The Carousel Shoppe" in *The Heartlands Today*

"When Sam Was Dying" in *The San Diego Writers Monthly*

"The Isle of Skye" in *Reader's Break*

"Lindsay Saturday" in *The Tucumcari Review*

"Triples" in *Still Waters Review*

"Fireflies" in *Sidewalks*

"The Girl On The Bus" in *The Flying Island*

The mind has landscapes which it is allowed to contemplate only for a certain space of time. In my life I had been like a painter climbing a road high above a lake, a view of which is denied to him by a curtain of rocks and trees. Suddenly through a gap in the curtain he sees the lake, its whole expanse is before him, he takes up his brushes. But already, the night is at hand, the night which will put an end to his painting and no dawn will follow.

Marcel Proust
Remembrance of Things Past

A Season
for Storms

There was this time in my life when it seemed all I could do was to put one foot in front of the other and keep slogging along like that all day until it was dark enough to go to bed. As I remember, the sleeping was the best part by far. Long hours of almost drugged sleep in which I lived in another man's body and awoke confused and ashamed in my own. That's what happens when somebody walks out on you. It's worse than being broke or sick. I know about those things, too, but getting dumped I think is worse. It hurts you in places you didn't even know you had.

When my father's family moved out to Illinois from the East, they stored all their worldly goods in an old warehouse while they were finding a house to rent. There was broom corn stored in another part of the warehouse and somebody torched it, trying to drive up the price of broom corn. So my grandparents lost everything, the beds and chairs and tables that would have been hard enough for them to replace out of their meager savings, but also the irreplaceable things like the photographs and mementos. I think I know how that must have felt because that's what my Lydia had done to me. She had torched me like that guy did the warehouse.

My restlessness was so overpowering, I was never comfortable in one place. I kept wanting to be anywhere but where I was, the next room, down the street, or miles away. When people tried to talk to me, unconsciously I'd keep edging away from them, just moving anywhere. So I quit my job and packed up my stuff and started driving. I can't say that really took me away from my grief, but at least I had the sense it was at my back. As long as I didn't stop for long, it couldn't really catch me.

I was moving then, aimlessly through northern California and Oregon and Washington. It was at the end of one of those days that I pulled the pickup off the road into a tiny little town up in the timber country. They had bulldozed a shelf back into the pines and a dozen or more scattered buildings had grown up there like wild mushrooms. Some clapboard houses, but mostly cabins and shacks and Quonset huts. One bore a neon sign in the shape of a cocktail glass and it was that I had noticed first from the highway.

Before I could reach the porch of this tavern, a rain, whose approach I had not suspected, came up out of nowhere. It picked up at a furious rate and was soon rattling in the tin downspout of the tavern and pounding on the brick-colored clay of the parking lot. So I came through the door, wheezing and stamping and shaking the water from my jacket and hair. The bartender looked up curiously from his efforts at moving some bottles from cardboard boxes to his shelves. "Got caught, did you?" he said, with a big smile. "That's the season for you. When you least suspect, down she comes. Come on in, my friend. It's warm by the bar. I got a space heater here."

I moved into what was really a large room that seemed much tighter because the wooden walls were as dark as if they were scorched. And it seemed every inch of space was covered with posters and photos and magazine clippings. Down one side was a pool table, with scoring beads hung above the worn felt and cue sticks neatly stored on the wall. A dozen tables crowded the other side where a silent jukebox hunched in the corner. In the shadows, a grizzled Labrador labored to his feet and ambled across the floor, his heavy body swaying from side to side. He disappeared through a curtain into a back room.

I took a place at the end of the bar near the red-hot elements of the heater. "Bar whiskey, please," I said, "with a short beer back." The rain had, if anything, intensified my thirst. The bartender quickly poured my drinks. As he pushed the glasses across the bar to me, he followed them with his large and callused hand. "Andy," he said. "Nice to have some company. What's your name?"

"Luke," I said, not knowing until that very second that I would be lying to this stranger. I did that sometimes in those days. I would be among new people and suddenly find I no longer wanted to be myself. Luke was a name I began using when Miller and Hawk Ryan and I started running the town girls when we were fifteen and thought it furtive and cool to have aliases. So, all my life I was Luke when I wanted to lie. And when he asked where I was from, I said Monterey, too, though really I was from Salinas. There was no mystery in this. All those things that had to do with Lydia that I could disavow helped push me away from her. So, let the lying begin, I thought.

"You be spending the night?" Andy asked me.

"If there's a greasy spoon around here. And a cheap motel."

"Well, we can fill that bill," he sighed. "The greasiest and the cheapest."

"Then I guess I can relax," I said, loosening my jacket and sprawling out on the stool. So Andy and I talked, he content I guess to have the company and I happily distracted by the creativity of my tales. It was as if I were meeting this Luke myself for the first time, fascinated with what he would say next. He was an interesting fellow. It turned out he had once been in combat, and some years ago he had been rich for a while as a wildcatter. But lately, he was mostly a drifter.

So contentedly engrossed was I in the conversation, and increasingly mellowed by the whiskey, I scarcely noticed that the door had opened and the woman had come in. But there she was, suddenly, right there at my side, asking Andy who his new friend was. As Andy introduced us, I turned, distracted from my running narrative of lies, and really saw her for the first time. She was shaking off and folding an umbrella, but some of the rain had caught and was gleaming in her hair, and a drop or two glistened on her pale forehead. Because she was a friend of Andy's, who in a short time had become one of Luke's dearest friends, I was sure happy to meet her. But I saw no beauty in her pale, hard features and felt no stirring for her. Her name I never did catch when Andy introduced us and so I never really knew.

She was a strange one. I guessed at first she was drunk or stoned. But then, I wasn't sure. She looked so directly at me through her dark eyes, that I wondered if I knew her and had forgotten where or when. But she gazed in the same intense, familiar way at Andy, too, and about the room, as though it were all new to her and incredibly interesting. I began to wonder if she was crazy.

From her face, I thought she was too old for me, although I sensed what I was seeing was so much experience, it made me feel like a little boy. I thought, if I had to guess her age, try as I might, I would probably guess too high. Her smile was tight-lipped, which I always assume means there's a problem with the teeth. But that thin smile had a guarded and mysterious quality. There also was a certain girlishness in the movement of her body that I was sure must still be attractive to some men.

I can't really account for the next few hours. I had been going about the business of getting drunk before she came in, and it was hard to pull back from that plan. I seemed to slide back and forth into a pleasant blackness, a vacuum of time. But I would pull up into the light occasionally and could see that she was sitting beside me at the bar, looking closely at me and smiling. It slowly dawned on me that we had been in some kind of conversation for awhile, and I wondered with a start who I had been in that talk, me or Luke? And where did I come from, Monterey or Salinas? The second thing, and this was strangest of all, this woman seemed to be interested in me. Since Lydia, I was convinced that I gave off an aura of defeat that isolated me from the world, most especially from women.

Looking back, when I recall that night, I can see with great clarity her face and her movements. And I remember well her bold familiarity. But I don't remember at all things she said. I mean other than what was necessary to go from one place to another. But in between all of that, anything that she might have told me about who she was or what she did or believed in, I simply can't reconstruct. All I remember was how she kept saying, "no, tell me about you."

I failed to reorder for awhile, suddenly wanting to be sober. She helped by ordering me first some coffee and then such a quantity of pretzels and chips that I soon lost what appetite I had. The fuzziness began to part and I struggled back among the living, to see what was happening there. My recovery I could see reflected in her face. She seemed pleased that I was coming around. Sensing her approval, I took another look at her and reassessed her looks in light of these feelings she was displaying for me. I admit I found much more there than I had seen before. "So, you like me?" she asked, laughing a little, still without showing her teeth. "Do you have someplace to stay tonight?"

"No, I was going to go to the motel."

"You can stay with me," she said, casually. "But we'd better go now. I'm getting tired. Why don't you pay Andy."

Tired, I thought. How could it be time for bed? I looked around the tavern and was surprised to see it had filled up with regulars. Somehow, the afternoon had become evening. Andy smiled weakly at me as I paid him. I sensed his disapproval that this woman and I had developed something for each other. I didn't care, I thought. Andy's jealousies were his problem. For the first time in a long time, I felt good about the way things were going.

Then we were in the rain and a cold wind that snapped me quite awake. Our feet splashed in the puddles in the parking lot. We tried unsuccessfully to keep her umbrella over our heads in the wind, and we stumbled in the dark. The woman laughed at it all. A hard laugh that I felt I had heard all my life.

It was good that I had sobered up, because in the rain and darkness, finding my footing on the rickety steps to her front porch took everything I could muster. But we managed somehow and entered a door she had left unlocked. She turned on the light to reveal a room of shabby furniture nearly covered with magazines that spilled carelessly over the chairs and floor. The air seemed trapped and rancid with mildew and cooking odors. A small television blinked on noiselessly in the corner, like a night light left burning. She took hold of my hand and led me into the bedroom.

The bed was scarcely made, a spread pulled up over the topology of tangled covers. Sleeping there were three cats, whose yellow eyes blinked open to watch us approach. And lying with them was a man. Fifty years old I'd say, if he was a day. I couldn't have been more surprised, that he was there at all and that he was so much older than her. His drawn, sleeping face wore a two-day white stubble, and his clothes were soiled and wrinkled. "Get up, all of you," the woman said sharply. "I got company."

And so they did, the cats sliding away as water on glass, from the bed to the floor and gone. The cat man, looking up with red eyes at us, his face offering no recognition. He stood up, shook his head to clear it of sleep and shuffled through the doorway. I heard his phlegmy cough echoing through the little house. The woman sighed, closed the door and locked it with a bolt. And then she came close to me and kissed me. I don't think I have ever known, in such a small and unexpected way, such total happiness. I found myself choking back tears.

She took off her things then, as immodestly as if she were alone, and cast them in different directions where other clothes were sprawled in disarray. As she did, she gestured to me to take off my clothes too, and I eagerly obeyed. But these I tucked in a small pile beside a chair.

Her breasts were as white and soft as her face was hard, and her smooth limbs reflected like polished marble the light from the bedside lamp. In fact, her slight body was so unexpectedly lovely I had to gasp. No baby's mouth had ever touched those dark nipples. I would swear on that. She moved gracefully as she smoothed out the bedclothes and tucked in the sheets. Then led me softly into the nest she had prepared. Made speechless by my good fortune, I settled down with her into a bed made warm by the cats. And the cat man.

Afterwards, I slept like an angel. Not drugged at all with sorrow as I had often known back then. I awakened once or twice in the night and sensed the woman's presence near me, a most comforting and reassuring feeling. In my quite vivid dreams, I was a child again, back in Illinois, with my parents both alive. I came in from play and found myself once more at the table in my mother's kitchen. Mom, Dad, Larry, everyone was there. And there was not a single moment in these dreams for my Lydia. As though she had never existed. When I awakened in the morning, incredibly refreshed, I smiled to myself in gratitude for the woman beside me and I reached for her and moved close to the heat coming off her body.

She stirred with a grunt, and turned her face to me, a face the morning light through the small panes of the window chose to treat most ruthlessly. I quickly reminded myself that this face was not what she was about. What I needed was to see again the dance of her remarkable body. To be once again the man I had been the night before. But the woman wanted nothing of my dreams and my gratitude. With a quiet oath, she turned fully from me and sought the outside edge of the bed, nearest the wall, where she could meet again with sleep.

I had no trouble finding my clothes, still bundled tightly by the chair. I dressed, shivering. A glance through the window showed that the storm had cleared. The surface of the puddles in the yard was unbroken with raindrops. I unfastened the bolt and slipped furtively through the door, not sure what I would do. Then a voice, as unexpected as if Lydia had suddenly called my name. "Want some coffee?" it said, and I turned my head and there was the cat man. Why would I not expect him there, I thought. I realized I had quite forgotten that he existed, amazing as that seems.

He stood in the doorway of the tiny kitchen, holding a cheap aluminum coffee pot, looking even more rumpled than the night before. One of the cats swirled about his legs. My new confidence made me terribly bold. I knew that I wasn't afraid of him at all. Yes, I would have some coffee, I thought. I moved past him into the kitchen. There was a small table by a window, covered with oil cloth. Another cat was sitting on its haunches squarely in the middle of the table by the sugar bowl and the salt and pepper shakers. I sat down and glowered at it until it moved sullenly away. The cat man put my cup before me, followed by a small carton of milk. He said nothing while I sipped my coffee, but I could smell his foul breath even at a distance, and I could feel his eyes upon me.

"What brought you here," he finally asked, dully.

I wrapped my hands around my cup to capture its warmth in the chilly room and thought for a moment, not sure what I wanted to tell him. "Just traveling," I said.

"And so you met Andy," he led on, "and so you met her."

"That's right," I said. "Just like you say."

A long period went by, in which neither of us said anything. I finished my coffee and set it down, with no offer from him to refill it. I wanted another, had to have another, and I resolved to go to the greasy spoon Andy had told me about and have a dozen cups if I wanted. This cat man wouldn't be deciding how many cups I could have.

Then, in a voice so strange and calm, without threat, it made the hair stand up on my arms, he said, "It's time for you to go."

I looked at him and he didn't turn away. His red eyes were set on mine.

"All right," I said as slowly as I could, determined not to show the slightest fear. "It's your house. So I'll go." I didn't truly know that it was his house. But suddenly, I had this twinge of uncertainty, like before I had met the woman. First, the way she had turned away from me that morning. Now the cat man, docile as he had been in the face of her commands, was starting to crowd me. It was almost as though it had been me lying on the couch through the night, listening to her moans of pleasure coming from the bedroom.

I started to rise, but his hand fell on my arm. "I don't know what you think," he said. "And I don't care. People like you have your lives. And I have mine."

I looked at him, not flinching from his steady, almost

crazy stare, determined not to tear myself away too quickly.
But, in a well-measured moment, I rose, thanked him for the
coffee and left him sitting at the table. The cat, apparently
relieved that I was leaving, quickly jumped up by the sugar
bowl again. Very quietly, I eased open the bedroom door and
saw that she still slept on in the heap of covers near the wall.
In my jacket, I found a piece of paper and a pencil, and I
wrote a note. I wished her a good morning and told her I
would be having some coffee at the diner Andy had told me
about and that she could join me there.

I left without speaking again to the cat man, and turning on the squeaking front porch steps, looked back at the
clapboard house where I had spent the night. Like the
woman's face, it hardly bloomed in the morning light. In
truth, there was almost a human quality in the way it stood
there in the mud, slumped and defeated. I walked back down
the lane through the little town, stopping momentarily at the
dark hulk of Andy's tavern, where the neon cocktail sign was
stilled and the window shades were drawn. Andy's big
Labrador was lying on the porch, his head resting heavily on
his paws and his eyes following me as I passed.

The little diner by the highway made things much better. The coffee was nice and strong, and the waitress there so
bubbly friendly, she was the perfect antidote for what I had
just been through. She brought me country sausage and eggs
and toast made from homemade bread. She leaned over the
counter while I ate and told me all about her life. She also
asked me about mine and I found myself largely telling the
truth. Then, the cadre of regulars began to trickle in, shop-
keepers and truck drivers and loggers. There was a lot to talk

about, the storm and how it seemed to have cleared off and where people were from and where they were going.

I'm normally not a very gregarious person, especially when I'm sober. But I found myself quite chatty and open that morning. I spoke to just about anyone who wanted to give me the time of day. How many cups of coffee I drank I cannot imagine. Except that I was fairly trembling with a caffeine rush. Then, I began to notice that some of the people were ordering hamburgers or the Special, which was meat loaf and mashed potatoes. I realized then that it was nearly noon. I never really expected her to show up, I thought. I'm not a complete fool.

But, I should say, a most remarkable thing occurred that week. At least for me. I finally had a day that was better than the one before. And then another to boot. As I drove down the highway between Klamath Falls and Redding one afternoon, I felt the stirrings of something like a kind of joy deep down inside me, as unexpected and scary as if it had been the first twinge of pain from a malignant tumor. I had to stop along the shoulder of the highway for awhile to contemplate it. Shortly after that, Luke and I had a falling out. It was inevitable I suppose. But one day he just slipped out of the cab of the truck and I never saw him again. I have no idea where he is now. For all I know, he might have wandered back to that little town in the logging country. Maybe he just had to have some kind of showdown with the cat man. That's Luke's problem now, I figure. It's sure not mine.

Whatever Happened to Grossfield?

He's disappeared somehow. When his high school class holds its reunions and publishes its breezy brochures, his classmates' lives are celebrated with their colleges and degrees, titles and accomplishments, hobbies, the names of their spouses and children, and their stated outlooks on life and aging. His biography offers only his name, "Lawrence Herman Grossfield." His old Army outfit, the 468th Transportation Battalion, has met every ten years since the Korean War. But they meet without him. Occasionally, someone who hates loose ends has tried to track him down. But the trail has become quite cold.

For one thing, Grossfield is far away, actually half a continent from his home town. He has lived for a long time in an old, inner-city neighborhood. It's a closed community, quite unlike the cookie cutter suburbs of the big cities, those encampments where he might have stayed visible. Then, he loses his job. "To cut costs . . . to make room for younger people," they tell him. So, for awhile, he tends to avoid contacts so he won't have to explain what has happened to him. To complete the process of disappearing, he simply outlives everyone he knows. Though he is only in his mid-sixties, Grossfield has outlasted Pete the barber and Trudy the manicurist and Mrs. Schilling who owned the grocery and Earl and Pete Townsend and Shorty Keller and the old man who sold vegetables door-to-door from a beat-up truck. And he has outlived all of his family, including his only brother in California. No letter has arrived in Grossfield's mail for years.

But we know Grossfield exists because there he sits on a park bench late on a September morning. A pale man in a dark gray suit that seems two sizes large for him. He looks perplexed at this moment because it has just occurred to him how the park has changed. Though the grass is mown regularly, it has seen little real tending of late from the city. The fountain and the wading pool and the band shell and the flower beds have been torn out. In their place is a small playground with whimsical structures, like a yellow elephant, whose trunk serves as a kid's slide, and a bright pink Cinderella's carriage.

Presently, Grossfield, though still obsessed with the changes, rises from his bench and begins ambling up Fullerton Street, a little commercial area once lined with stores of every description. There were two groceries, the Egyptian movie theater, Pete's Barber Shop, The Fairview Town Tavern, and William Browne's Appliance Store, where, in the early days of television, people stood on the sidewalk in front of the store window, watching the small, snowy images on the TV's. There was a candy store where freshly-made caramel apples were displayed on wax paper and a beauty shop where women sat in long rows under the shining domes of hair dryers, reading their magazines.

But all of that's gone now. The shadows of signs identifying those businesses are left on sooty walls, and the boarded-up buildings sit forlornly like untended gravestones. The streets seem larger to Grossfield, more open and spare. Trees have died and never been replaced. Even those careless little plots of green that squeeze in between old buildings and fill the summer air with the pungent junk smells of tree of heaven and ragweed, these too have disappeared. And the sounds are gone, the wisecracking, the shrieks of children, the dogs barking. No life seems to stir.

Suddenly, a black boy, a teenager, bursts out of an alley and pauses on the sidewalk. He wears baggy shorts that hang to his knees and enormous basketball shoes. His eyes, large and curious, gaze intently at Grossfield, making a prickle of fear go up his spine. But he begins to realize the boy is not looking at him, but actually through him. Abruptly, the boy yells an obscenity at someone to Grossfield's rear and rushes past him toward the park, his long, lean strides eating up the pavement.

"I'm hit!" Rodriguez screams from just in front of him. "Grossfield! Help me! The artillery rounds are falling in their bivouac area, the explosions, more felt than heard, throwing dirt everywhere, sending metal fragments stinging against the truck bodies. He hears Rodriguez's calls, but for the moment, all he can do is press his body directly into the ground as debris rains down on him. Abruptly, the shelling stops. He crawls forward cautiously to where Rodriguez lies and finds him rolled up in a fetal position, holding his shoulder. His face is ghastly pale. Grossfield tentatively checks the wound. It's a small hole out on the tip of the shoulder. The bleeding seems minimal.

"Come on. I'll help you down to the aid station," Grossfield says. Rodriguez's fear leaves him as they slowly walk along the road, through the chaos of all the units bivouacked in the draw in the dry hills. Everyone they pass is offering awed chatter about the shelling. "Hey, Grossfield," Rodriguez says, "is this a million-dollar wound, you think? The son of a bitch hurts enough for it."

"I don't think so," he replies. "I think they'll have you back by at least tomorrow. But look here. I got a piece too." He notices for the first time the neat little gouge on the back of his hand. There's quite a bit of blood (it's even dripping down on the road), but not even a trace of metal.

"Hey, Grossfield," Rodriguez says, "I bet we both get Purple Hearts for this. That'll be something to talk about."

The doctor at the aid station puts a couple of stitches in Grossfield's hand and takes down his name for the records. Maybe he will get a Purple Heart, he thinks. Rodriguez's wound, as it turns out, is a million dollar one, and he's loaded in an ambulance and sent back. So, when Grossfield is released from the aid station, he walks alone across the ruts in the road, the dust standing like powder, to where a field kitchen is set up on a hill. The grizzled cooks, who somehow look more like soldiers than the kids they keep sending up with the infantry, are standing by the tables in their aprons. Waiting expectantly, like diner owners in bad locations, they're serving steak today. Floured, fried round steak, hot and greasy in great steel bins. And there are mashed potatoes and gravy and canned sweet corn and fresh bread. Grossfield loads down a tray with food and finds a little shade behind a truck for his feast. And there he sits in total bliss, the flies buzzing benignly about him. As he eats, he watches the steady procession of trucks, filled with olive drab soldiers, heading up in the hastily deployed counteroffensive. Maybe all these troops are supposed to be enjoying this meal, he thinks. Steak day. That's always a big event. He chews slowly, the grease glistening on his chin, his Purple Heart wound throbbing only slightly.

It's time for lunch. Grossfield stops at the supermarket, a hulking old structure that now seems more dedicated to security than selling, its front windows protected with metal grating and its aisles observed by video cameras. He has food stamps to pay for pork and beans and a can of peaches. But this day he lingers at the meat counter and examines the packages of red meat gleaming under the neon lights. He's tempted to try cooking some but decides against it. On the hotplate in his little apartment, such meals remain as memories for weeks at a time.

Led by his hunger, he heads up Thornton, where he once had his own house. In those days, Thornton was a pretty little street with neatly-swept sidewalks and sober, white-painted houses under the canopy of oaks and maples. Old women moved back and forth in their porch swings, like metronomes measuring the slow passage of time.

In a few minutes, Grossfield arrives at his present place, above the drugstore, once owned by Frank Sills, now by a discount chain. He labors up the creaking wooden stairs, pauses to catch his breath, and walks down the gloomy hall to his room. He unlocks his door and steps inside, and it's there, in the shadows, that he sees the football coming at him. The ball is perfectly illuminated on all sides by the mercury vapor lights of the stadium. It's tan and pebbled leather with two white night game stripes and it spins in perfect spiral, like a slow motion rifle bullet, closer and closer. Grossfield awaits it like an old friend.

What a surprising thing that Johnson has taken a knock on the bean and has to come out of the game in the third quarter. Then the second string end, Ferretti, aggravates his bad knee. Only a few minutes are left in the game when the coach comes looking along the bench for him. The name "Grossfield" coming from Coach Henley's mouth, sounds very foreign. He puts on his helmet and moves, as in a dream, out to the huddle in the middle of the field where the players with muddied blue jerseys stand under the lights.

No one seems to notice him as he joins the huddle. Their faces are downcast from the licking they're taking. This final drive against Jefferson High's subs is the last chance to save any face at all. The huddle breaks and Grossfield moves tentatively to his position. The ball is snapped, and he runs mechanically on a pass route drilled into his head by three years of practices. He never expects to be thrown to. Why would they do that? But Phillips, the quarterback, dazed from being run down all evening by Jefferson's big linemen, isn't checking credentials. He breaks loose from a tackle, glimpses a clean blue jersey, and unloads. Grossfield sees the ball coming toward him, bright and shiny in the blackness. He has it, taken to his stomach like they told him repeatedly in practice not to do. You're supposed to take it in your hands, "little fingers together." But he catches it nevertheless. The defensive back blasts him hard, and he comes up slowly from the chewed-up turf. "First down," says the referee. "Way to go, Grossfield," another voice says.

He collapses in his only stuffed chair, never feeling nor hearing its ancient springs protest. The ball is tucked safely in his gut.

As moments pass, the lights over the field diminish. Emerging are the dark, somber shapes of his furniture, the piles of newspapers and paper sacks that cover every flat surface in his room. In a moment, he regains his strength and struggles to his feet to fix his lunch. The exertion of the first down catch has only intensified his hunger. He opens the cans and eats the peaches standing up while the beans are warming on the hotplate. His stomach feels better when it's full. He pulls the Murphy bed out of the wall and lies down on the rumpled pile of covers. Grossfield rubs his eyes, hearing the eyeballs click in their sockets. Then he becomes very still and quiet. He listens to the rattle of the sparse traffic on the street below, a man's cough in a nearby room, a scrape, a bump. And to the room itself, its sound, like a breathing.

That sound is reassuring to Grossfield. When he first hears it, he recognizes it from some time in his past, but it takes a long time to figure out where and when. Then, one day in a flash, he remembers it's the sound of the house where he grew up. That same rhythm, the movement of air. Those long days when there's nothing in particular to do from the time he opens his eyes until he's put into his bed at night. Only the passing of the sun, leaving its slowly-changing patterns of shadows on the walls. And the breathing, the slow, quiet breathing. After Grossfield figures it out, he feels much better about his room. Somehow, he has traveled in a great circle. The only chaos has been in the middle, when he worked, when he was in the Army, and when he once was married to a woman he can barely picture now. The time in the middle consumed most of his life, but now it seems like a mere flutter.

How Trudy the manicurist and he ever got together he cannot imagine. The after-hours Christmas party at Pete's Barber Shop where he often hung out. The bourbon and Coke they drank in his car. The touching. Who started that?

And then she is actually in his room, this very room. No, that isn't true. It's in his house on Thornton Street and it's easily thirty years ago. Trudy's much more experienced than he is. "Oh Jesus, stop!" he shrieks in warning. But it's too late. Trudy stays with him and then afterwards, with resignation, spits softly into Grossfield's dirty sheets. "Oh my God, I'm sorry, I'm sorry!" he pleads to her, clutching at her body in the darkness.

"Just as well," she says, giggling, drunkenly. "We got no protection. I'd a been sorry in the morning. So, what the hell, Grossfield . . . Merry Christmas."

He hears her voice very clearly, as though she's in his bed right now. But, in truth, Trudy has been gone for many years. More than just dead, he thinks, because no one's alive who ever knew her. No one, that is, but him.

Grossfield was a salesman in those days, representing a business forms and office supplies company. A respectable enough job, he figured, that a Trudy might be interested in him. His territory was this very neighborhood and a large part of the city beyond it. He had a car, but seldom used it, covering his route on foot or by bus. He carried a sample case of his wares, a large leather case which once was brand-new and eventually was sprung at the hinges and dog-eared at the corners. So many years he worked that route, but somehow it collapsed like a dwarf star in his memory to the proportions of a single day. A day in which he leaned against the counter at Solomon's Jewelers or Herkle's Flowers, talking and writing down the string of small orders that was his living. He actually sees himself in his suit and tie, smiling and telling his jokes.

Sometime, hours later, he awakens. He can tell by the shadows it's late in the afternoon. If he doesn't get up now, he'll surely be up bright-eyed at two or three in the morning. With his TV out of whack, that will never do. Grossfield reels to his sink on stiff, unsteady legs. He splashes water onto his face and rubs his cheeks briskly. Then, looking in his mirror, he carefully combs his thinning hair. He stares steadily at his own eyes and they stare back with curiosity. Now he shuffles over to the window and looks down at the street below, where an afternoon wind is pushing newspapers and dust along the gutter. Should he go out for a walk, he wonders. But the thought of trudging back up the stairs afterwards makes him hesitate. He sighs and turns around. And there, waiting for him, is the football.

"Grossfield?" the man in the dark suit asks. A thin woman, her face full of concern, is peering into the store manager's office.

"Yes, I'm Mrs. Grossfield," the woman says.

"We've got your boy here," the man says. "He was wandering around the Toy Department, looking for you."

Grossfield's eyes suddenly explode with hot tears as he bursts out of his chair and rushes into her arms. "I was lost," he sobs into the musty folds of her wool dress. "It's all right, honey babe," she consoles, rubbing his shoulders and smiling knowingly at the manager. "Mommy won't ever let you get lost again."

Ancient Lives

A nice surprise at the tourist center. In place of some chain concession snack bar, the government had licensed local Indians to sell these homemade corn tortillas wrapped around a kind of chili and bean concoction. Two women, their faces the shape and color of ripe persimmons, were working the stand, baking the tortillas on an iron grill set over a charcoal fire. They served them up on waxed paper along with a sweet tea they made, and we ate in a dark, little room of adobe walls and red tile floors. I liked the whole idea of this enterprise, including the uneven brownness of the tortillas. "Great stuff," I mumbled to Eileen, as I happily ate.

"If it has something to do with food," she replied, "you'll call it great."

"You're right," I agreed, pleased that our first conflict of the day could be on such a light subject.

After our impromptu late breakfast, we paid for our tickets and set out to climb up to the pueblo. Another pleasant surprise: instead of a stairway or elevator, there was only a bleached wooden ladder set up against the escarpment. That seemed to me to make the trip more of an adventure than just sightseeing. I had a little shiver of expectation. "Want me to go first?" I offered.

"No, let me. So you can catch me if I fall."

"Fair enough," I said, holding the ladder for her. Actually, it was so stout and well-anchored in the stony ground, there was really no need to steady it. So, I followed her on up the cliff, watching her climbing ahead, framed by a blue sky uncompromised by even a wisp of cloud. I was mesmerized by the movement of my wife's body, even in her loose-fitting khaki slacks and blouse. Her sturdy legs dug at the rungs and the hips she complained were becoming too broad of late shifted back and forth as she climbed. This motion made the subtle mound between her thighs appear then disappear with each stride, presenting it to me in a way I couldn't ignore even at such a platonic moment. Of late, such glimpses of her that I stole while she bathed or dressed or even climbed a ladder fully clothed, tended to remind me of all that was between us. Almost fifteen years we had been together, eleven of them as parents to our daughter. But one does forget sometimes, I thought, that we're not just business partners, presiding over our assets. We're man and woman. That's another thing entirely.

There were a few moments on the ladder when I think we each had a sense of height and possible risk, but we were soon to be rewarded for our efforts. At the top of the cliff, the air was cool and exquisitely sweet. We found ourselves on a barren plateau, nearly covered with the ruins of crude, straw-colored stone walls. Some of these were now no more than waist high, but the ranger down below had said they had all once been part of a structure of hundreds of rooms. Here and there on their impassive faces were dark windows like the eye holes in a skull.

Looking behind me, I was surprised to see how high we were. Out on the desert, I could make out only a single car on the road we had taken from Santa Fe. We were quite far away from anything or anyone and, for awhile, had the ruins to ourselves. The only thing stirring was a large bird high above I wanted to believe was an eagle.

We made our way first through various fissures to the center of the ruins. In the time when people had lived in the pueblo, there had been a central court or plaza, and its presence was still obvious. We sat on the crumbling remains of a wall and viewed the flat space spread out before us.

"Can you see them?" Eileen murmured.

"Yeah, I can. The old guys are sitting along this side, telling lies to each other. And smoking. Tobacco or something."

"'Something' is right. Probably stoned to the gills. Or at least they had some kind of booze. That's what men do. Right?"

"The women would be working," I countered. "Weaving at their looms, baking bread, washing. Such is the lot of women," I said, with a mock sigh.

"You can say that again. And I see dogs, lots of dogs. Mangy old dogs, sulking around with their tails hanging low."

"And kids everywhere," I offered. Chasing each other, running into the adults, being loud."

Eileen absently took my hand and squeezed it without meeting my eyes. I guessed immediately that gesture was about Ginny. Sorry I had drifted into that, I pressed her hand back firmly. Then she rose and pulled on my arm to get me to my feet. "Let's see what else is up here," she said.

We wandered for an hour or so, exploring the labyrinth of weathered walls and gazing out at the low, rugged mountains around us. It was all so lovely and peaceful. Fascinating, I thought, the presence of all those ancient people about us. The sense of their being, not profound, but ordinary, human. And now, vanished. Maybe the women at the stand below carried some strain of that old line. But essentially, they had been gone for thousands of years.

Eventually, we came to the entrance of a large hole cut deep into the hard, rocky surface, with a ladder descending into the darkness. Eileen checked the guidebook she had carried up in her bag and said it was a sacred place where only the medicine men were allowed to go. "What do you say?" I asked, "Do you want to go down there?" I was in a stage of my life where I was always trying to press the limits a little. I have no idea why. Maybe, at the moment, I was just showing off for my wife.

"I don't think that's a good idea," she answered. "It's probably full of spirits. Do you think it's wise to disturb them?"

"Eileen, these people couldn't even control their own destinies. Much less come here to affect ours."

"So, you're saying there couldn't be spirits here?

"Well . . . you're right."

"And what about Ginny? You just think Ginny's dead too. Like some . . . some cat that gets run over in the street."

"Sweetheart," I said patiently, "you know what I believe. I'm convinced Ginny's at peace. That seems to me like a pretty good thing." I was becoming afraid that Eileen was reeling out of control again and that even this promising day was at risk.

"At peace?" she asked mockingly. "So, you really don't think Ginny is . . . is in Heaven. She's not being Ginny at all. She's just some body . . . lying in her grave . . . some dead thing."

"I can't believe she's in Heaven because I don't . . ."

Eileen erupted before I could finish, pushing me in the chest so violently I nearly fell right into the hole and screaming in a voice that might have awakened the pueblo's former inhabitants. "Goddamn you! You would keep Ginny out of Heaven, wouldn't you? You and your atheistic bullshit! I hate you! I hate you! She then dissolved in racking sobs and grabbed hysterically at me. I managed to secure her arms and tried to calm her.

"Eileen, I can't help what I believe. And you can't really think I'm in charge of all this. You're having your own doubts, and there's nothing wrong with that. But don't blame me. Then she collapsed against me, and I held her tightly as she sobbed into my chest. How could there be so many tears? I had suspected I had heard her crying that morning, in the bath in our hotel room, while I was still half asleep. And now it had started again.

Eileen pulled away from me, not spitefully, but firmly, and wandered down a passageway through the ruins to a spot near the edge of the cliff, where she sat down on a stone facing out over the desert. I respected her distance, and sat down myself, some ten paces away. It was so quiet up there, nothing could be heard for awhile but Eileen's muffled sobbing. When that finally ended, there was no sound at all. At first it was just the absence of the constant racket that surrounds us most of the time, human voices and street traffic and aircraft overhead. Then the silence met a point of diminishing returns as the roar of the blood rushing through the veins of my eardrums became almost deafening. I tried humming a tune under my breath, just to drown out the sound of my own circulation.

From where I sat I could observe my wife quite clearly, for the air was so thin and clean everything seemed to stand out in crisp detail. I could see her pale, freckled hands resting on her legs and the way her hair blew in the gentle breeze, so that she instinctively reached up from time to time to push it back in place. A great wave of tenderness came over me. I realized, after all those years, how much I loved this little woman. I also knew she wouldn't be with me much longer. Ginny's death had shaken me to the core, but it had destroyed Eileen. "I just can't accept it," I had heard her tell her friends many times. This difference in the intensity of our grief was killing our marriage. No matter how many trips, like this one, we took. No matter how many counselors we saw together or priests Eileen consulted by herself, nothing would change. The strange virus that came looking for Ginny last November had found more than one victim.

There was something else, too. For some reason, I kept thinking of that line from our wedding ceremony, "What God has put together, let no man put asunder." Ironically, it seemed to me, it was God himself, Eileen's God, who was pulling our marriage apart. When things had been good, our beliefs, our differences, didn't seem to matter. Now they did.

What if she's right, I mused to myself. What if there really are spirits up here, and they're looking out on us right now from the shadows of their houses? What do they think of the lives and dreams of such frail modern mortals? To lose sons and daughters was commonplace to them. They probably lost one for every one raised. That must have hurt them too. But they went on, found food and water, made love in the late silence of the night. They took what they could from their short existence. To grapple and struggle with life as Eileen and I did would have been unthinkable to them. Eventually they were gone and it didn't matter anyway.

The sun was by now firmly established in that metallic blue sky, dispersing the chill on the top of the plateau. I felt its warmth ease the muscles in my limbs, and I hoped the same thing was happening to Eileen. There are only so many long nights in our lives, their dreary hours filled with our fears and our doubts. Then the day always comes around again. This one offered up a particularly glorious midmorning sun, maybe compared to any I had known in my life. It made all the things below, the red-streaked cliffs, the crumbled walls, seem to turn up their faces to be washed clean. I wanted desperately to believe it also was shining down on the cemetery where Ginny lay beneath what was still unsown soil. This was a dis-quieting place to Eileen. But to me it offered some consolation to picture my daughter still lying quietly below in her blue satin jumper and the blouse with the puffy white sleeves, her bangs combed from her pale forehead, the way her mother could seldom make her do. This vision was, admittedly, a poor substitute for my little girl, but I truly believed it was the only one I had. It would have to do.

Now, reason told me Ginny's grave was actually a thousand miles away in another climate where the forecasts had predicted three more days of spring rains. But still, in those ruins where we sat, I believed there was sunshine enough to cure all the madness and sorrow in the whole world. Even when I closed my eyes, the sun still was with me, a bright insistent orange behind my lids. It seemed to me, all of that sunshine flowed quietly down that morning, in peaceful, healing streams, on the plateau, the ruins, on everything that had ever been. On all those ancient lives. And, of course, on mine and Eileen's too.

THE
CAROUSEL
SHOPPE

In his thirty-ninth year, Bo Easley decided he wasn't getting anywhere. He had struggled for years as a second-rate general contractor, remodeling ramshackle buildings in an old village called Millerstown that had long ago been swallowed up by the fast-growing city. And that appeared to be the best he could do. It was true he had Penny, a wonderfully loving and loyal wife, two beautiful children, and a gang of friends who thought he was the greatest guy in Millerstown. But, as for the big dreams of his youth, well, forget it.

Then, something of a miracle occurred. Somebody got the idea that the old commercial area with its arched bridges over the canal and its cluster of small fieldstone buildings was reminiscent of maybe Brugge or Burton-On-Water. Though no relic existed from the miller's trade that gave the village its name, the locals began pushing the miller theme until mill wheels even graced the drawings of school children. And soon nearly everybody in that section of the city picked up on the illusion and wanted to live and work in romantic Ol' Millerstown.

The only thing was, when they began dreaming about the accouterments of a theme-driven neighborhood, all those boutiques and sidewalk cafes and artist's lofts with vaulted ceilings, there weren't many contractors who could deal with the sow's ear reality of Millerstown's real architecture. That was anything but classic. The exception was Bo. He had spent the past fifteen years, stoically working with the area's slipshod construction and cheap postwar fad materials, all that aluminum siding, tarpaper brick, fiberboard, glass brick and cement filigree. Only Bo seemed to cheerfully accept the fact that basements were supposed to flood, garage roofs to sag, walls to be papered and paneled in half-a-dozen layers, and windows painted shut. Only he seemed to be able to get in there, jack up that sloping floor and clean up that over-painted mantel without charging a king's ransom. So he was not only extremely busy, but the three spec. houses he was carrying and fixing up suddenly were worth a lot of money. Almost overnight, Bo Easley became, certainly in his terms, rich.

The remarkable thing, his friends said, was how little this shift in fortune seemed to change him. He bought a new car and some new clothes, but he still ran around most of the time in a T-shirt and blue jeans with his trademark White Sox cap, set well back on his head and a pencil stub stuck in the band. He did, in time, switch from beer to Scotch. And he moved his family out of the bungalow on Whitcomb to one of his rehabs along the canal, although they did need more space anyway. But, as his pal Tiger said, he seemed to be a man without a dream.

"No dream?" Bo muttered, as he fingered the last kernels in the bowl of popcorn that came with their drinks. They

were sitting in The Razzmatazz, one of the last of the old insti-
tutions on Canal Street. Everything else had gone, as Bo called
it, to cute. Cute tearooms and cafes and imported cheese shops.
Probably because it was such a quintessential neighborhood
tavern, The Razzmatazz had been spared the transition to cute,
and went on serving drinks in its own dark and corrupt way.
But there was something a little disturbing about the whole
thing, Bo thought. It was as though the cute people couldn't
just let it remain a bar. They now thought of it as an historical
treasure. "You're wrong, Tiger. I do have dreams."

"Oh yeah, name me one."

"Well, I'd like to screw Naomi Fletcher."

"See, that's exactly what I mean. That's no dream
'cause I think you could probably do that. In fact, she told me
as much."

"You're shittin' me."

"No. I told you she wanted to use you on her new
dress shop. But what I didn't say was the way she talked
about you. A guy can tell those things, you know. She's hot
for your bod, old buddy. But, you know, one thing surprises
me. I never thought of you as some guy who cheats on his old
lady. You ever do that?"

The stock male lie caught in Bo's throat. Then he slowly shook his head. "No, I never went out on Penny. Oh, there
was a little thing at a construction materials show about ten
years ago, but that was it. Still, Naomi might be another thing."

"Well, believe me, if that's what you want, you'll get
your chance."

"I've got a question," Bo said. "I've known Naomi for years, though not real well. So why is she suddenly so interested in me?"

"Jesus, Bo, don't you know? You're a success. Everybody knows that."

"You mean she's interested in my money?"

"No, no. She's got plenty of that herself. It's just that the world loves a winner."

After he said goodbye to Tiger that evening and headed home to supper, Bo felt a little regret. He was sorry he had told his friend about Naomi. He sure hadn't meant to do that. And he was sorry he had described his desire as "wanting to screw her." In his heart, it really was a loftier feeling than that. He should have at least made that clear.

Tiger was right about Naomi's remodeling job. Within a week Bo was standing in the latest vacant storefront she was developing into a new retail concept. The store, at present, seemed to be between illusions. The peeling murals of scenes from the Grand Canal still marked its days as an Italian deli. Now, Naomi had another idea. "It's a dress shop, Bo. I call it The Carousel Shoppe. The whole store'll be like a merry-go-round, with the horses on poles all around and garments hanging over them."

Bo was wandering around the space, baseball cap pushed back on his head, examining the heating outlets and switch boxes. He was having trouble looking Naomi in the face with his knowledge of what might be happening between them. But what he saw obliquely he liked very much. She was dressed in a very smart spring-weight suit, too smart maybe for Millerstown. Her long, auburn hair was pulled up on her head and her spike heels clicked like castanets on the tile floor. There were some who thought Naomi had a certain cheapness about her and wore too much makeup and jewelry. Bo thought only that she was so clean-looking. And certainly exciting.

He had thought about all this pretty carefully since his conversation with Tiger. It was true Penny meant a lot to him. Even though she had put on a few pounds since their dating days back in high school, he still liked to look at her and to make love to her. And he had always admired her sweet, unflappable cheerfulness. When he thought about his wife, images of warmth and unfettered closeness came to him. His feelings about Naomi were quite different. She seemed to be all the things that lay beyond his comfort zone, things that challenged him. She was frightening in a way. And that made her seem all the more desirable.

"Where'll you get the horses?" he asked.

"There's a place in Chicago that has stuff like that. Pretty expensive though."

"I got an idea, Naomi. A long time ago, there was a merry-go-round in Canal Park. I don't know why, but it's still stored in a shed there. It doesn't belong to the village and I think I know who to call about it. The price could be right. Like maybe nothing."

"But carousel horses are a big thing now. Doesn't anyone know what they're worth?"

"Don't count on the local big-wigs to know anything.

Now if this was a mill wheel or something that'd be different."

"Oh, Bo. That would be wonderful if we could get those horses. Maybe we could even put up a little plaque explaining where they came from. Or some old photos, if we could find them. You really are good. Like they say."

"Part of the service," he said, smiling and looking as directly as he dared at her.

The next day he met Naomi on the far side of Canal Park and led her through a grove of maples to the dilapidated lattice shed where the carousel was entombed. He produced a key for the laminated lock and as the door, nearly broken away at the hinges, scraped open in the cool dirt, they both peered into a darkness rich with the smell of decay. As their eyes adjusted, objects began to appear like the images in darkroom pans. Beneath the dust and grime, they could see a smiling clown face on the carousel's facade and the cymbals and percussion instruments that once carried part of the old ride's sweet-sad melody. The horses themselves, frozen in wide-eyed hysteria, were stacked up like cord wood. "Ah," breathed Naomi, her trash-to-treasures sensibilities aroused by the find, "it's perfect."

She turned toward Bo and he saw her eyes sparkling in the gloom of the shed. He noticed distinctly at that moment the murmur of the bumblebees in the tall weeds outside and the infield chatter from the distant park ball field. And he felt, as though she were naked, the presence of her body. Somehow, they had wound up standing very close to each other among the piles of litter. And if Bo was going to balk at this critical moment, Naomi knew better. She gathered his confused head, baseball cap and all, in her insistent arms, and her tongue was soon thrust well into his mouth.

In the days to follow, Bo conceded that his wildest dreams seemed to be coming true. Still, the next steps seemed very tricky. Millerstown was like a fishbowl. He couldn't just start hanging around with Naomi in local bars. And he certainly couldn't go to the little cottage where she lived off of Canal Street. As they tried to make plans, the careless euphoria of the lattice shed was gone. He felt the icy prickles of fear quite clearly up his spine. How do other guys do this, he thought. It was a scary process to pursue this prize, with his marriage and everything he knew and loved held hostage.

He was with Naomi a lot as the horses were mounted on poles around the shop, each at a different height to simulate a real merry-go-round. Bo thought it was strange seeing these relics from the shed in the clean, freshly-painted store. Badly water-stained and their paint nearly chipped off, they looked like decomposed corpses in a morgue. The portion of the facade that had been claimed was even worse. In life it had been brightly painted and gilded, bedecked with gleaming mirrors and carved cherubs. In its present condition it resembled more the gate to a neglected crypt. In this odd, ghostly setting, the sight of Naomi's body as she walked about, her perfume trailing tantalizingly behind her, made Bo's head spin and kept him tethered to his dangerous dream. "But not here, Bo, for God's sake," she insisted. There's not even carpet yet. Don't you want it to be special the first time?"

After a week of such dancing around, it was she who came up with the plan. She reserved a room at the Family Motor Inn, a high-rise, reasonably-priced hotel five blocks off the commercial area. He was to meet her there the next evening. He certainly could do that safely. No one he knew ever hung around that hotel. The only catch was that he had to stay the night. She was adamant about that.

"Penny, I have to go to Chicago for that special trim I told you about. I was thinking, as long as I'm there, I might look up Sid and catch a Sox game. So, I'll probably just spend the night."

The lie was out of him, much as he imagined through all the rehearsals, and though he couldn't breathe for the moment, he felt like it had eased out casual and believable. He was busy pretending to be concerned about a door frame in his own house, frowning and jiggling it with his hand, so he couldn't see Penny's eyes on him. He hadn't been away from her in years, even for one night, so this was a big announcement. In the pause that followed, he imagined her thoughts. He anticipated the sudden inspiration she might have to join him, quickly dashed by her remembering the inevitable babysitting problems. The question of trust itself would be considered too. But there, Bo reasoned, he had a great backlog of reliability behind him and she knew it. "Whatever you think, honey," she finally said. "You deserve a little fun."

Bo had only to get through the day. In Naomi's shop, the horses had been stripped to the bare wood and prepped by a crew of craftsmen Bo had recommended. He couldn't quite say why, but there was something beautifully primal and true about the way they looked in their natural wood grains. The next week the artist was scheduled to arrive to begin painting them, and he wondered if that was really the thing to do. Bo watched Naomi moving gracefully around and through the horses with her swatches of fabric and her paint chips, her face cracked with a frown of intensity. He was nearly overcome with desire. But by late afternoon, the lust was equally mixed with fear. He was, supposed to be in Chicago by that time. So he fully expected Penny to appear any moment at the plate glass window and to know the whole sordid scheme. Even if all this came off without a hitch, he wondered if he could be worthy of a "real woman" like Naomi. It had been many years since he had been to bed with anyone but Penny, and even there, he was well aware of how his wife accommodated his sexual clumsiness and inconsistencies.

At four they closed up the store, and waving cheerily goodbye to each other to fool any spectators, they parted. Naomi to her hotel room to "freshen up," he to O'Toole's, a little out-of-the way alley bar, for a bracer. There, he dawdled with his drink, resolved not to get sloshy and mess up this great moment. By then, his nerves were such that O'Toole himself asked him what was the matter, and he found he had to visit the men's room twice at the bar and once more in the lobby of the hotel. In the elevator going up to her room, he had such doubts and fears for his competency with this woman of his dreams that his stomach was tied in knots.

There is perhaps some sub-cult of fatalism that declares no tragedy pre-conceived can ever occur. By that doctrine, Bo had certainly explored so thoroughly the terrain of discovery, failure and disappointment, he left no room for anything but success. And when his scented goddess came to him in bed, all eyes and mouth and breasts and legs, he was all he had prayed he'd be at the moment of truth. In fact, later, over the champagne she had chilled in the room's plastic ice bowl, she managed to remark, "Well Bo, you're a handy man in more ways than I'd dreamed."

But then he awakened in the middle of the night, hungover and shaken, totally unable to sleep. And, to his horror, in the first light of dawn, he discovered he could actually see the back of his own house from the balcony. Though a dozen blocks away by car, it was as the crow flies, no more than a quarter mile. He could clearly make out his garbage can, his kids' swing set, the big yard thermometer mounted on the crab apple tree. He was struck dumb with remorse and loneliness and could barely make it through the room-service breakfast and Naomi's requested last tumble in their befouled sheets. Her body, that the night before he saw only as a tender vacuum he was born to fill, now repulsed him as though they were in a reversed magnetic field. As he finally pulled away, spent but unsatisfied, she easily noticed the difference. "Oh Bo," she said, raising up on her elbows over him, her pale, blue-veined breasts falling on his chest, "I'm afraid I've lost you already."

It was true. When he kissed her goodbye that morning, it was for the last time. He went home to Penny like the prodigal son, and began treating his wife in a way that made her remark the next day to her friend Janice that she was going to send Bo to Chicago more often. For a few weeks, he

lived in stark terror that he would still be found out, but when
it became clear that wasn't going to happen, he realized just
what a great life he had and how foolish he was to risk it. He
had a good job that gave him the sense of "seeing something
finished" as he put it. And when it was time to relax, he could
just throw some steaks on the grill and hang out with Penny
and the kids. What more could I want, he thought.

Naomi wisely realized things had probably turned out
the way they were meant to be. She always figured Bo had
more potential as a friend than a lover anyway. She was right.
He even stayed on as her contractor, through the Carousel
Dress Shoppe project and some of her subsequent brain-
storms like the Things Of The Orient and The Brideshead
Bridal Boutique. With his lingering guilt about running out
on Naomi after the night in the motor hotel, he donated a
large part of his services free to her, certainly for blueprint
consultations and crawling around beneath the floors of this
place or that, probing with his screwdriver for suspected dry
rot. She, good businesswoman that she was, happily accepted
this charity.

As for The Carousel Shoppe itself, it was to be a great
success for many years. Naomi had a certain eye for fashion
and the needs of her customers. And the store itself was pure
panache. Even when it was closed for the evening, men and
women alike would stop on the sidewalk and gaze wistfully
through the glass at the tableau within, in lighting as soft and
pink as cotton candy. They would marvel at the beautifully-
lacquered horses and the gilded merry-go-round facade from

Canal Park, faithfully restored by the best of Millerstown's artisans. "It sure takes you back, doesn't it?" they'd say. "Oh boy, what excitement."

Instincts

The ringing phone, his daughter's sobbing voice, the familiar feeling of being yanked out of his comfortable world and into the hysteria of hers. Well, here we go again, Danny thought. One more time I'm on the road, heading out to find Stacy to try to pull her out of still another mess. Slowly, he inched his way through the five o'clock traffic of San Francisco and Oakland, grumbling to himself all the way. Even when the traffic thinned, he knew he still had a long way to go, and nearly two hours passed before he finally rolled through the tree-lined streets of Stockton.

As he neared the area where Stacy had told him she lived, the neighborhoods grew less attractive. No big trees softened the sullen shapes of tract houses and banged-up old cars in the driveways. Why, no matter where she lived, did Stacy seem to gravitate to this kind of squalor, he wondered. Was it just a lack of money? Or was there still a childish rebellion in there somewhere? If Mom and Dad liked clean and pretty things, well then, she'd just try something else.

It was hard to find the exact house because few people marked their property with numbers, as though ashamed to admit this was really where they lived. But, in time, he located a down-in-the-mouth stucco bungalow he thought was the right one. There was no car in the driveway, so he assumed Stacy's new boyfriend was away. Just as well, he thought.

It was fully dark now as Danny parked his car and picked his way through a clutter of flower pots and car parts and what looked like the remains of a lawn swing. An emaciated cat screamed menacingly at his feet and then slipped noiselessly into the darkness.

Danny rapped his knuckles against the aluminum screen door, making a terrible, metallic racket. Almost immediately, Stacy called out in a breathless voice, "Come in, Daddy," as though he had to be quickly stopped from disturbing the entire neighborhood. Danny stepped into a darkened room where a window air-conditioner struggled noisily. The only light appeared to originate in a distant kitchen. Stacy was crouched barefoot on a sofa, looking very small and childlike and visible only in silhouette. As he approached her, she sprang up to kiss him and accept his hug, and then retreated to her original spot as though on a string. "I love you, Daddy," she said, making Danny feel instantly ill at ease, because the words usually preceded a request for something from him.

He sat down on a straight chair across from her, still trying to make her out. "What's the matter?" he asked, "why can't we have some light?"

She sighed and said, "I'm not sure that's such a good idea." He pushed himself up and managed to find the chain to the table lamp beside the sofa. When the harsh light snapped on, he noticed she was cheating one side of her face away from him. When he brusquely took her chin in his hand and turned it around, he could see the dark bruise under her eye and her swollen lip. "Jesus Christ, Stacy. Not again." Not the most sympathetic remark, he had to admit, but it was how he honestly felt.

Danny sat down, trying to control his rage. The room that had been revealed by the light was so depressing, he almost wanted to plunge it back into the more bearable darkness. The peeling wallpaper and grimy windows seemed to frame Stacy like the coat of a bag lady. She had cut pictures from magazines to hang on the walls. Images of lithe fashion models cavorting on beaches and clinging to the rigging of yachts. Rock stars and socialites photographed at glamorous parties. That was the storybook life Stacy always aspired to, but wound up instead in rooms like this one.

And there was always something worse that he'd imagine, bad as this seemed to be. Some drug business, some sex business. The dark, stickiness that always followed Stacy from one hovel, one horrible companion, to another. Who was this person sitting before him? It had become one of the central questions of his life. Was she some living proof of his weaknesses?

His daughter reached into a purse, pulled out a cigarette and lit it with a plastic lighter. He hated seeing her smoke. It always seemed to him a ritual designed to accentuate the distance between them. "Stacy, why can't you leave this? Come home with me and we'll see if we can work something out." He was trying very hard to be calm.

"You always say that, Daddy. I just can't leave."

"Why not, sweetie? Give me one reason."

"You just never get it," she whimpered. She hung her head and her long, dark hair fell down and covered her face. Her shoulders were shaking as she began to cry. He sat silently watching her, aware that once he would have run right to her and held her in his arms, done anything he could to stop her tears.

"Stacy," he said, searching in himself for a gentleness he thought more appropriate to the moment, "have you talked to your mother? Does she know how things are?"

"Mom and I have trouble talking," Stacy sniffed through her hands.

"When did that happen? I thought you were always so close."

"We were. I don't think so anymore."

He shook his head. "I don't understand."

She wiped her face on a sleeve as her weeping subsided. Danny stood up, took out his handkerchief and handed it to her. "I don't know if this is true," she sniffed, "but since you guys broke up, I think she kind of blames me for some of it."

"That's crazy. You were long out of the house when we had our trouble." This seemed like a thing he had to say to his daughter, even though what she related was probably true. In the long run, Stacy's crazy exploits had cut deeply into what he and Sadie had together. They had even gone through the humiliation and expense of a major drug charge against her and had saved her from prison by inches. It wasn't as though either blamed the other for what had happened. But, eventually it was hard to look at a person who had shared so much suffering with you and think of anything positive.

"Sometimes, I really do wonder if I could have done more for you," he said. "If I'd been more supportive, made you understand how much I love you."

"Well, we're only human, Daddy."

Secretly, Danny was hoping Stacy would let him off the hook a little, but it didn't seem likely. "That's the damned trouble," he said. "We're only human, but then we get these consciences that keep making us pay for 'only being human.'"

"That's a sweet thought, Daddy," she sighed.

Danny was sorry she had said that, because as he finished his little speech, he realized it was mostly contrived. He couldn't remember ever actually wishing he had done more. My God, he thought, am I just stumbling headlong toward being a first class windbag? Some old fart, always blowing off some pious horseshit.

"What you don't seem to understand is this," she began, "about the only thing I have going for me right now is the sense that I'm kind of in charge. I'm a grownup, you know. A stupid, non-functioning grownup maybe. But still a grownup. Then you or Mom come along and tell me I'm wrong about that, too. You see things much clearer than I do. And you've got a better way to handle things. Just what does that leave me?"

"It's part of the job, honey. It's hard for me to see you in something like this," he said, his arm sweeping to indicate the house and everything connected with it.

Stacy abruptly blew her nose into his handkerchief, sniffed once more with finality and turned her dark eyes on him as though seeing him for the first time. "Listen Daddy, I want you to understand something. I really love you. I love you for getting on your white horse and galloping over here to save me from all these terrible dragons and everything. I really do appreciate that you care like that. But I'm not going back with you. I'm going to settle things with Bryce. I'm going to figure out what I'm going to do next. And all of that I'm going to do by myself."

"I hear you," he said. "But, there are just some things I can do to make it easier for you. I . . . "

"I don't want it easier, Daddy. I want it my way, even if it's the hard way."

"Then, I guess I don't understand why you call me in the first place. If you don't want my help, why bother?"

"I have no idea why I do that. Maybe it's just a habit."

"Or maybe you actually do want my help."

They were so engaged in this standoff, both were totally surprised to hear a rattle at the door. "Oh God, oh God!" Stacy said, instantly alert. As somebody so accustomed to discord, she was always expecting it. "Oh God, Daddy. Please don't make trouble."

"Now, you don't understand," he said as he quickly

stood up and eased back into the corner of the room least visible from the door. "The trouble's already here."

There was a moment before the screen door rattled again, when nothing happened. A long, silent time, with only the monotonous drone of the air-conditioner to mark its passage. And then, a figure appeared in the room. He was tall and angular with reddish-blond hair above a pale and pockmarked face that was especially homely, Danny thought, even for Stacy's strange tastes. Only a single, long dangling earring, he perceived, marked this night bird as anything with a point of view. Earrings Danny couldn't like, but at least it said something. All the rest was the stuff of bus terminal waiting rooms. A face you'd forget the moment you saw it.

The young man was startled, wide-eyed. "Bryce . . . this is my dad," Stacy stammered. Danny was amazed to see Bryce absorb this news and struggle for some kind of composure. Then his shoulders began to relax and he started to smile. As though they might simply shake hands and exchange pleasantries about baseball or something. Maybe he'd offer the old man a beer. Sit down and shoot the shit awhile. Danny couldn't stand to see this young man feeling comfortable. "Did you forget something, pal?" he said. "Maybe you oughta fix the other side of her face, so she matches."

Of all the expressions Bryce could have chosen for the moment, he flashed up what amounted to a smirk. Stacy knew what that meant even before Danny could read it and react. "Please Daddy," she said, almost in a whisper. He couldn't even remember crossing the room or the movement of his hand. He only was aware, to his horror, that the first punch, delivered in a blind rage, totally whiffed. The very sick essence of a nightmare of impotence. But in breaking through nothing but thin air, its rush was so violent, Bryce's eyes snapped open, wide and terrified, and he froze in his tracks. The next three punches, delivered in tight with his thick body putting everything into them, landed hard in the younger man's mid-section. Bryce was pinned against the door, and Danny hit him twice more in the head before he crumpled to the floor.

By then, Stacy had scrambled across the room and was pulling at her father's jacket and screaming hysterically. Danny laid off for a second, breathing harder than he thought was probably good for him. Bryce slowly gathered himself together and came up to a crouch. His nose was bleeding profusely, but judging by the way he held himself, the shots to the body seemed to have caused the most damage. Maybe I busted a rib, Danny thought, gleeful at the prospect. As Bryce eased open the screen door and attempted to squeeze out into the night, Danny smashed the heel of his hand hard against the aluminum frame, making another fearful rattle. But the door was so flimsy and tinny, it bounced right off the fleeing young man.

There was a considerable banging and clattering outside as Bryce ran the gauntlet of the junk in the yard. Danny closed the door and leaned against it, fighting to catch his breath, feeling in a moment of panic that he was going to pass out. A darkness fluttered over his eyes, and he had to force himself back from it. Stacy was sobbing hysterically.

"Listen," he gasped, "I think you ought to go back with me tonight."

"Are you kidding? After what you did? Why do you do things like that, Daddy?"

"Instincts," he muttered, relieved that he seemed to be recovering. "Sometimes it's okay to go to the instincts." Danny tried another tack. "Look, a man my age shouldn't do stuff like that. I feel kind of funny . . . you know, dizzy. I'd rather not drive by myself back home. Please come with me."

For awhile she said nothing as she paced back and forth in the little living room, but she seemed to be calming down. Then, as she wiped the tears away with the back of her hand, she slowly murmured, "Okay, Daddy." For a moment, he wasn't sure he had actually heard her agree. "Let me get my stuff," she said, finally.

She shuffled into the bedroom, turned on a naked ceiling bulb and began throwing her few possessions together. Danny sat down on the sofa for the moment, cautiously evaluating his condition, checking his pulse, making sure he was going to be all right. In a few minutes, she brought out an old cardboard box full of her things, as well as a full laundry bag and some clothes on hangers. Between them, they took everything out to the car in only one trip. She didn't even bother to turn out the bedroom light or to close the front door.

He loaded her gear in the trunk, everything all ragtag. A couple of items fell out of the box and he had to look around for them in the dark under the bumper. Somehow, he knew all this stuff by heart. The bikini panties he would soon find hanging all over his bathroom. The contraceptives she would leave lying carelessly about, devices that Danny always suspected were the kinds doctors said were unreliable or dangerous. The packs of cigarettes. She waited in the car for him as he finished loading and never turned to look at him, as he settled into the seat, making the car rock hard on its shocks. He pulled away into the darkness.

She was quiet for awhile, but when they were on the highway she sighed and said, "Deja vu. How many times have you driven me back to your place in the middle of the night? Just like this."

He looked at her, somewhat surprised that she no longer seemed to be angry with him. "I don't know. Sometimes you wouldn't come. You'd get stubborn."

"My Daddy. My fucking knight in shining armor."

"I wonder if I'll ever get used to hearing that word come out of your mouth."

"Sorry. Sorry for everything."

"You don't have to apologize," he said, wearily. "I'm trying to understand what's bothering you. Maybe some of this is my fault."

"You think that sounds real humble and understanding, don't you? Can't you see how arrogant you're being? It's like you have such an influence on . . . on everything . . . that whatever's wrong just has to be your fault. Maybe, just once, you could see that other people have some say in things."

He was aghast at her remark. It was such a blindingly

accurate shot that instantly he could see it as very plausible. My God, he thought, I've fought so hard for control of my own life, maybe I just don't know when to quit.

Stacy leaned her head back on the seat. The conversation lapsed, and in a minute he heard her breathing becoming deeper as she drifted into sleep. As for Danny, he felt more relaxed than he had in some time. Like some business had been handled properly for once. As to the validity of Stacy's last words, he would just have to save that for tomorrow. Enough introspection for this night.

Stacy still slept on when they neared West Oakland, heading for the Bay Bridge, and joined back in the quick, nervous pressure of traffic on what the media called the MacArthur Maze. Below them, in the dark streets, Danny knew prowled such a dangerous crowd as to make Bryce seem like a Boy Scout. To his left, somewhere out there, was the blunt end of the Cypress Overpass where several blocks of the collapsed span had been removed. Danny always shivered when he passed it, remembering all the nights, coming home from A's games at the Coliseum, he had rumbled through the lower deck. The very place where, in the first minutes of the big earthquake, 47 people had died right there in their crushed cars.

Danny was very tired, but he was still able to concentrate on the highway ahead of him. At least on this particular night he thought everything was going to be okay. Through all those shadows, past and present, he drove his sleeping daughter home.

WHEN SAM WAS DYING

The day my Sam came back from the clinic and told me he had cancer, a profound change came over me. I remember thinking, if Sam can be as brave and noble as he appears to be, I ought to try to move it up a notch, too. Isn't it funny how much control we have when we really want it? Like a lot of old married couples, Sam and I had been moving steadily apart for years. But when I started into my noble act, I found myself not only admiring him, but loving him just like in the old days.

So, the first thing I did was to go see this guy Roger I'd been sleeping with of late and tell him I was dumping him. That was the easy part, even though Roger had that kind of cold, careless quality we admire in people who don't really belong to us. I'll admit he could make me wet and crazy like Sam never did. But it was real easy to leave him, almost therapeutic. I can still see that glazed, stunned look in his eyes and his funny little smile that I'd learned had nothing to do with anything humorous. Or decent for that matter. I liked it that there was nothing he could say about our parting, under the circumstances. It was almost like it was something to be proud about, that my husband was dying.

So then Sam and I got started on the business of keeping him alive. The cancer was in his colon, another one of those bad surprises that has something to do with money. I mean, along with all the other hundreds of things that didn't get done when money was tight, if Sam had gone in for regular check-ups, they'd have found the tumor in plenty of time. Rectal cancer is pretty easy to cure if they get it early. But yes, once again Sam and I fucked up. Just like we did by not fixing the roof before it rotted, and not buying that lot on the South Side when it was dirt cheap, and all the other things we didn't do right.

In fact, there seemed to be a lot of chickens coming home to roost about then. I mean, I really wished Sam and I hadn't pissed away almost every dime we ever made, plus even that little bit Momma had left me. Sam was no big shot, but he had been selling tools and stuff to factories in three states for years, and he brought home some pretty decent commission checks. So, where was all that money when we needed it? I also would have liked some more good friends or family to help me hold together. But old hothead me, I hadn't spoken to my sister Mary Alice in five years. And I'd just got through blowing off my best girlfriend Janet, over some kind of bullshit. But listen, what did all that mean next to Sam getting cancer?

Oh yes, there was our daughter Julie to think about. She had just finished her junior year at the state college and had gone off for the summer to work at Glacier Park over in Montana. Now, you'd have thought I would have grabbed the phone first thing and told her to get home and be with her mother and father. But long ago I'd stopped thinking about Julie as someone trapped in a small town like we lived in and in the kind of life Sam and I were leading. She was about the best student we'd ever had in our family and a real nice, straight kind of kid. We paid her way to school even when it pinched us a lot. And we didn't bother her much with our problems, even as big a problem as this one. So I didn't pick up that phone. And, in the weeks ahead, I found it gave me a little comfort to know Julie was running around in her shorts, in some clean-smelling woods, being a good girl I hoped. Instead of breathing hospital smells every day with me.

As for Sam, I don't think he was worried so much about dying as the fact the cancer was in his ass. For all his weaknesses, he was a proud man. The doctors had told him how far the tumor had gone and just what the odds were with the chemotherapy and the radiation and all. But most of all, Sam knew that whatever happened, people were going to be looking up his rear end and sticking things up there for the rest of his life. No matter how short or long that life was going to be.

But God, was he brave, my Sam. His face was just as composed and manly as John Wayne's had ever been in the movies. He went to his tests and his treatments without a single whimper. And at night, he'd reach over and start rubbing my back, knowing I was lying there wide-eyed, even though I was real quiet. And while he rubbed me, he'd say, "Now listen, Kitty, this is going to be all right. And if it doesn't turn out the way we want it, we just have to figure it's the way He wants it." Of course, the He part meant Sam had gotten religion after this thing started. Not at some crazy level, but in the way most terribly sick people do.

I wouldn't say anything when he did that. I'd just lie there and let him rub my back. Thankful that I had him there at all. You see, I'd already decided that when Sam was gone, I wasn't ever going back to Roger or any asshole like him ever again. I wasn't even going to look for a good man, as if there's a bunch of them out there anyway. I was going to be like my Aunt Sissy who lost her husband when she was still young and lived alone the rest of her life. Just going regularly to church, even on Sunday evenings. And seeing all the new movies that came out at the neighborhood theater with her girl friends. To hell with all that hormone thing. I was going to be like a monument to my Sam. Somebody around to remind everyone what a fine and brave guy he had been.

The clinic was over on Drexler Boulevard, a pretty, one-story brick building with a nice, big green lawn. It was a real open and sunny place, with porches and patios off the main corridors and waiting rooms. So patients and their families could step outdoors and see the flowers in the formal garden and hear the bees and be able to stroll around a bit. Those are all good things when you've got a lot of worry in your life and time on your hands waiting for things to happen.

So all through that summer, I'd drive Sam over to the clinic and I'd start waiting, while he was being tested and treated. I was working nights then as a hostess over at the restaurant. So I had my days free just to wait for Sam and try to talk to the doctors, always imagining there was more to the story than they were telling him. Those were long days for me, but how the hell could I complain when Sam was going through what he was? Throwing up all the time from the chemo and having tubes stuck up his poor ass. He lost so much weight you could count every bone in his skinny little body and see the outlines of a lot of his insides you'd never think you'd see. He even lost what little hair he had left.

Every so often, a doc would come out to the waiting room to see me, with his face all set and grave. I knew that look real well. There was just one thing after another they had to tell me. First the surgery. It was too late to do some kind of real cosmetic thing. They had to do a colostomy. So, at best, Sam would be going around with a bag full of shit fastened to his belly the rest of his life. Then they weren't so sure they'd contained the cancer in the intestinal wall or that the radiation and the chemo were doing the job. Not so good, they said, but still they could probably do this thing and that thing and blah, blah, blah.

Finally, one afternoon, after we came back from the clinic, Sam was resting while I was putting on my makeup in the bathroom, getting ready to go to the restaurant. I heard him calling my name and I went in and sat on the bed. It was September by that time so it was starting to get dark early. I could barely see Sam's face lying there because we hadn't turned on any lights in the house, the way you sometimes do even though it's dark. Especially that time of year when you have a need to pretend it will always be summer.

"Listen," Sam said, very slowly, "I want to talk about something. And I want you to listen carefully and not say anything 'til I'm finished. Okay?"

"Sure, honey," I said, not sure what was coming.

"This isn't going so hot, I mean the clinic and all. And that's okay if it's the Lord's will. It's not the dying that's bothering me. But you know we haven't got that much health insurance. And I don't think I'll ever feel good enough to go out on the road again. Besides, nobody's gonna buy something from a guy who looks like a skeleton."

"Honey . . . I started, hardly able to keep my tears back."

"You shut up like I told you," he said, "'til I'm finished." And so I did. "Now about the only smart thing I ever did was to buy that extra life insurance when Julie started college. Thank the Lord I did that.

"But the thing is, if I make it through a lot more time, and I'm not working, and we keep running into debt on the doctor bills, that money won't help. What I think is I've got to check out pretty soon . . . so there'll be enough for Julie to stay at school and you to . . . "

"No, no. Are you crazy?" I said, becoming hysterical.

"Goddamn it, let me finish," he said firmly. "There's just one problem. I checked that policy the other day and they got some kind of limitation on it. If I did something . . . I mean like suicide . . . you don't get the benefits. So I got to find some way to go out that doesn't look like I killed myself."

"I see. Okay, is that all you were going to say?"

"Yes, I guess," he sighed.

"Sam, my sweet, sweet baby," I said, climbing up on the bed and gathering his frail little body in my arms, "you're not going to commit suicide, obvious or not. Do you think I could go on living and have any kind of happiness, knowing you'd died to make that happen?"

"I was a fool to tell you, Kitty."

"No, you don't get it baby," I said, "this isn't about doing things for your family. You always were a good husband to me and a wonderful father to Julie. And you made all kinds of sacrifices for us even when you had to go without things yourself. No, your debts are all clear. If you have to die, and I'm not saying you will 'cause I think they're still going to get you well, you can die knowing you did everything you could for your family. And, if the worst thing does happen, we want every last day you can give us no matter what it costs to keep you around."

"I think that'd be terrible," he said," to squander away that money and leave you with nothing."

"No, you still don't get it. What I want as a favor from you is to give me a chance to make things up to you. I want to feel good about that because frankly I don't think the account's very close to balanced. Jesus Christ, I've been a lousy wife to you for years."

A great quiet came over the room at that point, so that I could suddenly hear the trucks over on the Interstate as though they hadn't been there before. "Baby, could I ask you something?" he said, "and you can tell me the truth 'cause everything is good with us right now. Nothing in the past can change that. Will you promise to tell me the truth?" His voice was very calm and even, so I knew he meant what he was saying.

"Sure," I said.

"Have you ever been unfaithful to me? And I mean, I really want to know, and I can take anything you say."

"No, Sam," I said," my voice as steady as a damned boulder. "God knows we've had our problems and sometimes I got real down on your program. But never has there been anything wrong . . . in that way, I mean . . . that'd send me out to another man." It's hard to tell about these things, but I think

I really pulled that off. My heart didn't start bumping around so that he'd feel it. And I think, even if he'd seen my face in daylight, there'd been nothing in my expression to give me away. Still, I was thankful for the darkness. Confident that I was in control, I added, "you know, you've been a road salesman all your life. You ever cheat on me?"

He was silent for a minute. Then he said, "I ain't saying." And I heard a murmur of the only real chuckle to escape that scrawny body in months. I laughed, too, out of a real kind of happiness. And I hugged my man as hard as he'd let me.

The next weeks somehow slipped by. I had trouble seeing time then in any kind of normal way. But it was most surely deep fall now. October. Always a funny season for me anyway. Some people don't like autumn at all, never forgetting for a minute that winter is behind, and that it is, after all, a season of dying. But I've never been like that. I love the colors and the mellowness of it. That sweet, musty smell of leaves and ripe apples. But still, my daddy died in the fall. And some years before, a man I thought I loved very much left me around mid-October, and I had to walk through the dry, yellow leaves along Lincoln Avenue, feeling all that hurting inside and not able to tell anybody about it.

So, you can imagine how I felt, going through this period with Sam as the leaves turned wonderful colors and began falling everywhere. And on one particularly glorious morning, just warm enough that the door was open out to the patio behind the visitor's lounge, I was sitting there quietly with Sam, holding his hand and talking about Julie and good times we had all had, when Dr. Pitzner came walking toward us down the hall.

I was so used to that grave, concerned look on a doctor's face, that, at first, I didn't even recognize the change. But, as he approached, I kind of started and then stood up, leaving Sam still sitting in his chair. "Sit down," Dr. Pitzner said softly as he motioned me to take my seat, "I want to talk to you two." He pulled another one of those tubular steel chairs over to sit near us, even though it was too heavy for that kind of spontaneous arranging and he had to kind of grunt with the effort. He pulled up the stethoscope that was dangling out of his white lab coat pocket, like a girl gathering her skirts to sit down. And he sat there kind of primly, as he talked to us, balancing a clipboard on his knees, and reaching up from time to time, to push back his horn-rimmed glasses that kept slipping forward on his nose. It wasn't the time to be thinking of something like this, but I remember looking at him, fussing around like he was, and thinking that's the kind of man I'd never go to bed with, even if he was a doc.

"I think I have some good news for you," he said, smiling only a little bit, as though it was very important for him to maintain his poise. "We seem to be getting control of the secondaries."

"You mean . . . " I gasped.

"Yes, Sam could just be in remission. But I don't think so. I think we've finally got all of it."

Sam was totally buttoned up, so I had to pursue this all by myself, awkwardly, stumbling. I felt like the time I won a TV set as a door prize at a lodge party and had nervously scanned through that long string of numbers on my ticket, wondering, as each one matched up to the number they were announcing, if my luck would continue. "You got all of it," I babbled, "you think Sam is cured?"

"There is good reason to hope," the doctor said. "A month ago, I wouldn't have thought it possible. Not in something that had gone this long."

"The bag . . . ," my Sam stammered in a hoarse voice, "will I have to keep the bag?" This seemed to me a crazy thing to say. I had become accustomed to the bag on his belly that had long ago become a given. I was worrying about life and death, not bags. Of course, it wasn't me that was wearing it. But then Sam grasped the situation and said, "of course, that's not so much if I'm going to live."

"You're damned right," Dr. Pitzer said, standing up and snapping his clipboard under his arm. He obviously didn't have to wear the bag either. "Now listen," we're going to cut back on the chemo. But we'll have to watch things pretty carefully. So I want you to call in tomorrow and we'll work up a new schedule. Okay?" The doctor had his fun with us for the moment, and I could tell his mind was drifting on to other things, his face getting grave again for somebody else's problems. To tell you the truth, that's the kind of brush-off I can take. As I watched him walking quickly away from us down the gleaming hallway to his next appointment, slightly splay-footed in his stride, I suddenly felt Sam's delicate hand on my arm. "My God, Kitty, did I hear him right?"

You can just bet that we totally lost it. I bent down and gathered that sweet little man, bruised veins, plastic shit bag and all into my arms, and we had such a happy cry together as I have never had in all my life. I mean it all came apart with violent, heaving sobs and enough tears to ruin my silk blouse. And we were still rocking and crying and holding on to each other as we walked out the front door of the clinic. The receptionist and half a dozen waiting patients watched us go with concerned faces at what bad news we must have borne to make us cry like that.

I couldn't help it. On the way home, I insisted we stop at Herbie's over on Second Street to celebrate, even though it wasn't even noon yet. Sam's stomach wasn't up to a drink, but we sat in the big leather booth back in the corner and he sipped at an orange juice and watched me put down two big Margaritas. That was enough, at that hour, to make my head spin and make the light through the plate glass window seem very strange and bright.

And then Sam made me start crying again, when he lifted his orange juice and said, "here's to you, Kitty. You're the one who pulled me through. Not those docs."

"Oh Sam," I said, holding his hand tightly and looking deep in his eyes, "you know what we must do? We must never let this moment get away from us."

"What do you mean?"

"I mean we should never get small again. We should always remember how important it is just to be alive. And have someone to love."

That's not easy to do," he said, between the careful sips of his juice. Sam had been queasy so long getting anything down was a major challenge. "We're only human. As time goes on, we'll get distracted by the little shit. It's easy to forget about keeping the moment." Isn't it funny what hope does to people. Sam had gotten kind of dull, almost stupid, when he thought he was dying. Now suddenly, he was a damned philosopher.

"Yeah, Sam, that's the easy thing to do. But we're not going to do it. We're going to get up every damned morning and try real hard to remember what we felt like, right here in Herbie's, getting drunk and loving each other. We're gonna be huuuge people!"

Sam laughed then, a hesitant chuckle like he was learning how to do it for the first time And he raised his empty glass to mine as though desperately proud he had managed to down the contents. "To Goddamned life, Kitty. To life . . . and to us."

And it turned out Sam was wrong. I mean with his doubts. As it happened we were able to keep hold of that moment even when the everyday crap started crowding in. We called each other "honey" and "sweetie" and we kissed a lot, just about every day. And when one of us got bitchy or fucked-up, the other would bring up that time at Herbie's and we'd smile at each other and remember. No, not for a lifetime, but for at least five long years. Eventually, Julie finished school and got married and Sam and I were grandparents. And Sam got back on the road and had kind of a rebirth of his career. And this time he didn't have all the expenses bogging him down, so he got to spend his money on booze and fishing trips and all that. And he was happy, I think. He used to brag to people about how at least his mid-life crisis had been a real one. And eventually he got so independent he wasn't so damned thoughtful to me as he had been.

That was okay. In fact, it made it easier, because I started sleeping with the manager at the restaurant, and later on, with this cop, who wasn't much more than a kid. A little sex, some cocktails, a trashy book to read on the slow days . . . how much more do you need in life?

So, Sam and I eventually drifted apart after all. But, I don't think either one of us believed that proved something bad. The point is, we did have those five years and the extra couple months before that when Sam was dying. I have this real clear memory of what kind of human being I had been and what I had done when I really tried hard. Talk about your finest hour. I was a giant.

MARCIE'S
VISIT

"I have a surprise," Ma said. "Marcie's coming home tomorrow." I looked up quickly at her from my eager labors on a pork chop. We all did. Pop, his knowing pursed lips indicating that for once he was in on the secret. Grandma, with her perpetual frightened rabbit look. And of course my older brother Paul, his eyes rolling to Ma in curiosity and his mouth full of mashed potatoes. I can still see Ma at the end of the table, her small, strong hands holding on to the corners of the tablecloth, like a magician ready to pull it out with our food-laden plates standing intact. It's hard to believe my country has fought four wars since that moment.

What a gift memory is. Of late, it works for me like that hard beam of concentration a drunk driver uses to stay awake. So, I take my time when I'm recalling something, willing to stop and sop up every detail, and always surprised there's so damned much material. For instance, I can piece together everything in that somber dining room and the parlor beyond Ma's generous bulk. The russet and brown still life prints of ripe fruit. The hand-crocheted doilies that adorned every chair and the bowls full of marbles on the tables. The mantel clock ticking solemnly.

Paul was first to gain his voice after Ma's unexpected announcement, forcing down the potatoes to sputter, "Marcie, here? You mean for good?"

Ma slowly shook her head. "No, it's just supposed to be for a few days," and then in a whisper she added, "but you can't tell."

"Oh, sweet Jesus," Grandma exclaimed aloud," her face full of fear. In fairness to that poor old lady, she was probably the only one honest enough to show the apprehension we all felt.

"Well, when does this happen," I asked, trying to appear calm about it all.

"Tomorrow," Ma said. "We have to pick her up at one."

We fell silently to our dinner then while she talked about how wonderful it would be to have Marcie around again. When we were all finished, the plates scraped so clean of every vestige of gravy you'd have thought they'd been washed, she disappeared for awhile to some secret place in the parlor and returned with three somewhat limp cigarettes. These she dispensed with ceremony to her three men and we soon were happily producing a blue haze in the room. Grandma put her lace handkerchief to her face in silent protest. The nightly cigarette ritual was a sure sign of the Depression that had hit our little household pretty hard. Pop had lost his dry goods store, Grandma her own house, and Paul and I (both college graduates and Paul nearing thirty) worked only an occasional part-time job or not at all. Ma too had suffered in the transition. In better times she had dressed much nicer and had a cleaning woman to keep up the house.

"Where will Marcie sleep?" Paul asked.

"I want you boys to give her your room," Ma said. "You can sleep in the parlor." Frankly, the idea appealed to me. At the time, Paul and I shared a double bed in our old room, hating the arrangement as just about all men do. On the parlor floor, I could keep some distance from my brother's cruel elbows and knees.

"We'll just have to do what we can while she's here," Ma added. "And that goes for you too, Grandma. Let's make her feel welcome."

"Well, if you ask me . . . " Grandma began, "she's in the best place she can be." But even Grandma knew her place, and she clammed up when Ma shot her a reproachful look. The cigarettes finished and put out with resigned sighs, we got up from the table.

"Where you going tonight, Paul?" I asked my brother on the stair.

"It's Friday, isn't it," he snapped. "I'm going downtown."

"Sounds good," I said, "could you lend me two bits for a movie?"

"You haven't paid me back for last time," Paul shot back. Then with a sigh and a shrug worthy of Barrymore, he added, "but let's go." At the time, Paul's part-time delivery job easily trumped my totally unemployed state. So, I certainly knew my place. I had to accept patronizing from Paul, and from Ma too, if I wanted their charity. But, as I remember, coming up with money for the weekends was about the worst of my status. You see, I had a secret I kept from all of them. I was the only one in the house not choking on the despair of the times. I have to admit I enjoyed being a man of leisure.

And so Paul and I set out to walk downtown. I'm sure we were like all young men of any era, probably sensing sexual adventure in the early dusk of a Friday night. Signals that always proved false. We were dressed, I recall, in the impractical formal fashion of the day, sporting ties and straw hats and white shirts that Ma had boiled and starched stiff as cardboard. It was a pleasant walk. Our street fed into a boulevard where we strolled slowly under the branches of cool, lush Dutch elms.

Paul stayed silent for much of the long walk until we reached the theater district on East Randall where, in those days, there was a great confluence of overhead trolley wires and tracks, and five movie houses brightened up the night with the color and hysterical movement of their marquee lights. The Alhambra. The Lowes. The Egyptian. The Regal. The Uptown. All with their double features, short subjects, newsreel and cartoon. Not many new movies escaped me in those days even if Ma or Paul had to provide the quarters. And sometimes I even caught the vaudeville acts at the Alhambra, sitting close to the pit band, laughing like a fool at the comedians and marveling at the jugglers.

Paul suddenly pulled back my arm and said, "Look up there. See who's going into The Egyptian?"

"Yeah. Isn't that Mary O'Brien? I don't know the other one."

"That's Vona Simmons. Goddamn, would I like to get a piece of her."

"Well hell," I said, "let's go say hello."

"No," he insisted, "let 'em buy their tickets first and we'll catch up in the lobby. I haven't got enough for all of us."

So we waited until the girls were past the ticket window and then suddenly appeared out of the night, so to speak, all white teeth and boiled shirts, tipping our hats and imagining we were oozing charm. Apparently, the girls never guessed our ruse and greeted us warmly. Suavely, Paul maneuvered our little party into the back of the balcony, and there, fell on Vona like a crazed tomcat. I knew Mary O'Brien pretty well as a good Catholic girl whose mother knew my mother. I had little reason to expect anything so I didn't even try. I wisely saw my role, in light of my subsidized status, was to keep Mary content with clever, whispered banter about the film so she wouldn't try to talk to Vona.

After the show, we went out on the street. There was a great gang of guys we knew, hanging out in front of the Tip Top, a new toasted sandwich shop, gawking at the cars, punching each other on the arm and telling jokes. Paul made his move and somehow got Vona to accompany him back into the alley. In what I knew was all too short a time, he returned looking a little surly. Shortly after that, Vona and Mary made excuses and sauntered off down the sidewalk, apparently restless for something that wasn't happening on that corner. "Hey Paul," one of the guys asked, "how'd you do?"

"Ah, not much," Paul said, which we all knew meant nothing at all. "Goddamn, I wish I had a car. How you gonna get somethin' in an alley?"

"Well look," I said, my timing almost non-existent, "I know I owe you for the movie, but how about a toasted cheese in here?"

"Bullshit," he fired back. "Get yourself a damned job if you want to spend money." With that he headed out, probably to sulk all the way home. I was resolved not to have my evening spoiled by Paul's moods, so I hung around on the corner another hour or so. Later, I borrowed a streetcar token from Charlie Mendenhall and saved the walk back.

Paul was already asleep in our stifling bedroom when I arrived. Quietly, I undressed and slipped onto the sheet, very conscious of the mythical border at the midpoint of the small bed. Paul was putting out quite a bit of heat and I hated being there with him. I guess somewhere in the night, I committed some kind of border incident by flailing out my arm in my sleep. At any rate, I awakened to a flash of light and terrible pain. Paul had smashed me full on the nose with his fist.

There was suddenly much commotion as we snarled and snapped at each other, the lights on as I clamored to the dresser mirror to see to my throbbing and profusely bleeding nose. I was half thinking of killing him, and I'm sure he thought the bloody nose was better than I deserved. Then we saw Pop standing in the doorway, sadly blinking at the spectacle before him.

"Sorry Pop," Paul sniffed. "We didn't mean to wake you. Everything's okay."

"Yes, I can see that by your brother's nose," Pop said. "I'm ashamed of you two. With your sister coming home, don't you think you could act like gentlemen? Just once?"

"Sure Pop," I said, feeling guilty myself, despite the fact that I was the injured party. "Just go back to sleep. We're sorry." Pop turned away, slowly shaking his head. I cleaned up the blood and eventually everything quieted down.

By the time I awakened on Saturday morning and stumbled down to the kitchen, the rest of the family had already had breakfast. I looked in the refrigerator and found half of one of Ma's fresh cherry pies, which was my idea of the ideal breakfast anyway. My nose, I noted happily, didn't feel all that sore, and I was in a fine Saturday morning mood.

I had one regular chore to dismiss, the cutting of Pop's rich bluegrass. In that time, the job had to be done with an awkward and heavy iron hand mower. I got right on the job, muscling the mower around the cherry tree, the fish pond and the bird bath. Ma looked up at me from where she was working in her begonia bed on the shady north side of the house. "Now remember, we're going to leave to pick up Marcie at one sharp," she called above the whirring of the lawn mower blades.

"Hey Ma, I can't go. We've got a game. Paul too."

"My stars," she sighed. "Nothing's more important than some dumb baseball game?"

"They're counting on us, Ma." I continued to force the unwilling mower into the lush turf.

"Well, you come right home," she insisted. "And I want you and Paul to be especially nice to Marcie. Make her feel welcome."

"Oh sure, I said.

After I finished the lawn, Grandma asked me to hose down the front porch so it would be cool enough for her to sit out there, which she loved to do. I ran the hose on the cement floor until the steam stopped rising and it was nice and damp and cool. Then she installed herself on the swing and worked on her needlepoint with her lips mumbling snatches of hymns. By that time, the sun was fully up and hot as Hell. The kind of day when dogs walk slowly down the street with their ears hanging down. I perched up on the porch rail and looked dully out at the street, listening to the monotony of the neighbor's kids' rope jumping song dueling with Grandma's trembling voice as she attacked "Little Brown Church in the Vale" and "What a Friend We Have in Jesus."

By then it was time to dress for the game. I went up into the heat of our bedroom and changed into my uniform with Rayner's Garage stitched on the back. I paused for a moment in front of the mirror as I gripped and swung an imaginary bat, thinking of what I wanted to do that day at the plate. This is what I really am, I thought. A ballplayer. That's better than being a law clerk any day. Even in the yellowed snapshots from those days, I still think I look pretty good. My jaw firm. My uniform very official looking. In front of the mirror, I set my cap just so on my head in the manner of Gehrig.

We played, like everyone else, in Fairview Park, where there were dozens of baseball diamonds laid out in a mosaic with outfields joining outfields. That concept could be a problem when somebody else's home run came bouncing through your infield during a crucial play. People came to see the games too, as though there was little else for them to do. They would sit stoically in the rickety bleachers, watching our infielders botch routine grounders, and they would throw their nickels and dimes into the blanket we passed around at the end of the game.

They say the real ballplayers come through in hot weather like that, when those flannel uniforms stick to your sweaty body. Yeah, I'd remember that afternoon real well even if it wasn't the day of Marcie's visit. Standing in the outfield, watching the heat shimmers rising off the infield dirt and smelling that sweet grass. Our pitcher was pretty good, so there wasn't much to do out there but think clean thoughts. I was hot at the dish that day, too, if I do say so. I went three for four, including a triple I legged out and slid in just under the throw. In the ninth, I raced way back almost to Baxter Avenue and snagged one in my outstretched glove that was at least a two-bagger and would have driven in the tying run. Everybody was real complimentary to me afterwards. Even Paul. We walked slowly home across the baked out diamonds, now empty and silent and crossed with long shadows.

No one was around when we arrived at the house. We both cleaned up in the basement where Pop had rigged up a "shower bath," as he called it, with a garden hose running into a gallon can punched full of holes and hung from a ceiling pipe. It was the only shower we had in those days, but it worked okay. I imagined Gehrig never felt better after he played a double-header against the Sox and emerged from the clubhouse shower. We had just finished dressing and were walking downstairs from our bedroom, when we heard them all coming up on the porch.

I saw Marcie for the first time, kind of in silhouette, when Pop helped her through the door. She was groping her way slowly and tentatively as though the reason she had been away was some orthopedic trouble. Then my sister stepped into the light in the parlor and I was struck dumb. She seemed much taller than I remembered. And she was smiling, with her brown eyes so sparkling wet I was surprised there were no tears on her cheeks. She was damned beautiful, though helped in no way by her white dress which even I knew was years out of style. And strangest of all, she wore on her feet Indian moccasins, more of the souvenir stand variety than anything authentic. And they reminded me that Marcie was still a patient and just on loan to us.

Thank God Paul had the sense to rush up to her and kiss and hug her or I'd have stood there all night figuring out what to do. So then I put my arms around her frail little shoulders and kissed her on the cheek. Her face was cool.

"I'm sorry you weren't here," she said, her voice measured and soft. "We had a nice ride." Pop and Ma and Grandma smiled and nodded ascent. "We even drove by Pop's store," she added brightly, which made Ma's face fall.

"Now Marcie," she gently chastised, "you know we told you Pop doesn't have that store anymore." But Marcie didn't even notice her and turned eagerly to me.

"Sonny," she said," how's the law going?" That stunned me. I desperately glanced at Ma, looking for help.

"Marcie," she said, "your brother had to drop out of law school and come back to help us here. So he's not really a lawyer yet." I smiled weakly, hearing for the first time this way of looking at my situation and frankly liking the sound of it.

"But Paul's still an architect?" Marcie asked, looking fondly at our older brother. She seemed sure he wouldn't disappoint her.

"No, Marcie," Ma said. "Paul is helping us too. You see honey, the country's in a Depression, so we're all sticking together."

"Well, are the boys helping at Pop's store?" Marcie was still trying to make it work out.

"Say," Pop interrupted, "it's too hot in here. Let's sit out on the porch." So, we all settled down outside with Marcie given the honored seat in the swing with Ma. Pop and Grandma took the two porch chairs and Paul and I sat on the rail.

Being on the porch didn't distract Marcie, and she continued to talk about Pop's store. Lovingly she described the bolts of brightly printed cloth, the racks full of ready to wear clothes. The bins of ribbons and trays of cheap costume jewelry. We all began to listen closely, hypnotized by her voice, even starting to believe her. I could see the store she described pretty clearly, with Pa standing proudly at the cash register and Paul and I bringing up stock from the back room and waiting on customers.

And then Marcie took another turn. "Did you know Banjo was coming over?" she asked brightly. "It'll be so good to see him."

A minute later, when Ma went in to start dinner, she motioned me to follow her. Standing in the hot kitchen, I started to babble about the absurdity of it all, but Ma shook her head with finality. "Never mind," she said, "why don't you go see if Banjo can join us after dinner."

"But Ma," I protested, "Banjo's got another girl now. He hasn't seen Marcie in years."

"Well, she can't seem to accept that. Just see what you can do."

So I slipped out through the back screen door and went over to Banjo's house. Luckily I found him outside, holding a hose on a flower bed. He looked up and said, "hey, I heard you won the game today."

"I had a good one," I replied humbly. "Say Banjo, did you know Marcie was home?"

His face tightened and, almost guiltily, he looked through the back door of his house to see if his family was hearing this. "No, I didn't. How is she?"

"Ma was wondering if you could drop by after dinner. Just to visit."

Well, to tell the truth, it took a little more persuading than that, but Banjo did finally drop by. He was an alright kind of guy. But I remember how sorry I felt for him when he came up on the porch that night. I mean, he must have wanted to do something. Or say something to her, more than comments about how hot it was. But all he could say was, "you look great, Marcie."

Marcie acted coy and even a little hard-to-get as if she and Banjo were still high school sweethearts. Of course, she still prattled on about the store and from time to time about what great careers Paul and I were on. Meanwhile, Ma, a little more relaxed with Banjo there distracting Marcie, looked up and down the street to see what the neighbors were doing. Just like any night. Pop, from time to time would get up and spit over the rail into the shrubs. It was a nice, purple summer night. The moths rioted on the street light globes. And the car traffic from Main Street hissed softly in our ears. In time, a clean white summer moon rose over the roof peaks and made the Chinese elms in our front yard throw ghostly shadows on the lawn.

Banjo and Marcie went inside to the parlor. I could look through the screen door and see them together. He had pulled a chair up close to hers and was talking quietly to her and gesturing a lot. He kept touching his hand to his shirt front as though he was introducing himself for the first time. She sat in Ma's dark red, brocaded chair, her feet demurely together and her hands in her lap. There was just a trace of color in her cheeks now and still that strange little smile on her lips. Occasionally, she nodded at what he was saying.

Once I went up to the bathroom, and on the way back, paused at the window on the hall landing. I could see Banjo heading out through the back yard and then down the cinder alley beyond. I guess he had wisely avoided running the front porch gauntlet. After he was out of sight, I heard footsteps on the stair. Marcie and Ma working their way up slowly. Ma's voice in a whisper saying something to my sister like "yes, sweetheart. It's all very nice." Paul and I laid the quilts and sheets on the floor of the parlor and I could feel that the downstairs was becoming much cooler and was happy to be there. The house was dark then. Silent. Paul rolled over and soon his breath found rhythm. But I lay quietly awake for a long time. Sometime in the night I heard, or rather felt, the texture of a woman's crying coming through the walls. Concerned at first that it was Marcie and that maybe I should do something. Then I realized it was Ma and there was nothing I could do.

Strange to say Marcie and I are all that's left from that Saturday night and that includes the house and the whole block that's now part of an interstate turnoff. Not that I'm doing all that well. My ticker's like an old furnace you hope will get you through one more winter. But, I'm alive. And as for her, she left our house in a day or two and never came back. For years, we all went to see her fairly often. But after Grandma, Pop and Ma and Paul were gone, their partings spaced out evenly across the years, I found it hard to make the trip to visit her and to look into those dark, liquid eyes that didn't seem to recognize me anymore.

I have always thought of Marcie as a kind of window to my past, the way back to times that were happy for me. But today my sister and I grow old in separate worlds, and I haven't seen her in more than twenty years. Still, when I think about Marcie late at night, in those terrible hours around two or three when you can't sleep and wonder if you're going to be around in the morning, somehow I feel like I'm closer to her than ever before.

THE ISLE OF SKYE

Danny assumed he would never sleep with Margaret. That was just the way things had worked out. It was true they occasionally hugged and kissed with what might pass for passion, but there was usually a touch of burlesque in those encounters. One of them would start wisecracking even though their mouths were pressed together, and they soon would break apart laughing. The problem was, they had become very close friends long before the opportunity ever arose for them to be lovers. And Danny figured if you lost the timing like that, it was pretty hard to regain.

There was something else, too. He had never made love to a woman as old as Margaret and he was not exactly comfortable with the idea. His sex life, such as it was since his divorce from Sadie, still was focused on younger women. Like Kelly, with her easy, vocal orgasms and Claudia with her strip queen breasts.

It wasn't that he particularly liked the company of these younger women. Their inexperience in other matters bored him. And he grew tired of their arrogance. They tended to use a man like him, hitting him up for a little money from time to time or confiding details of their love lives, past and present, he would just as soon not hear. In return, he supposed he exploited them a bit too, using their considerable physical charms to maintain his flagging libido. Danny was so fond of endlessly stroking and touching their bodies, mesmerized by the tactile wonder of it all, that sometimes they would complain.

Margaret was twice as old as Kelly or Claudia (of course, he had to concede, she still was a little younger than he was). She was attractive enough, even handsome, and certainly not stuffy. But, a lot older. When he thought about the prospect of Margaret's naked body, which he had never actually seen, he remembered as a boy, catching glimpses of his grandmother as she undressed for bed on those times he had stayed at her house. A peek of discolored and wrinkled flesh that had haunted his dreams all his life. Could he function in the presence of that? Even if his own belly sagged over his belt these days, when he wasn't consciously holding it in, somehow, to Danny, this seemed like a different matter.

No, if there was a natural order to his universe, it was this: he would continue to have sex with the youngsters while he could. And he would continue to keep Margaret as a special kind of friend and confidante. It was possible, he thought, that their relationship was helped by the fact they never slept together.

Margaret had a kind of loyalty that went beyond the usual. He appreciated the way his enemies automatically became hers. He even liked the instinctive, motherly way she was always picking lint off his clothes and adjusting his hair like he was being readied for the camera. Or maybe more basic, like a primate grooming ritual. And he couldn't remember a time when he was sick or just plain down that Margaret was too busy to help out. That, he knew, didn't necessarily come with a sexual relationship.

But Danny's life had never stayed on a pre-ordained course. And one afternoon, a major shift began with no more notice than a ringing phone in his law office on California Street. Pushing aside the accumulated pile of briefs and notes on his desk, he groped furiously for the phone as though it were the last outrage of a particularly bad day. A series of problems on an impending trial combined with a bad scene with his daughter had taken their toll. His impatient grunt into the receiver would probably have chased away all but the most determined caller. "Danny, this is Margaret," the startled voice on the line said, "are you all right?"

"Oh hi, sweetheart," he replied. "Sorry. It's just one of those days."

"It's Wednesday. Are we still on for tonight?"

He glanced at his desk calendar where he had scribbled Margaret's name as a reminder of their ritual weekly dinner? "Oh yeah," he stumbled. "Look, maybe we should . . . "

"Come on Danny. If we have to get in good moods for dinner, we'd both starve. You know you can lick your wounds in front of me."

Somehow the metaphor made him laugh. "But is wound-licking at the dinner table good manners? What would you say if your kids did that?"

"See, you're better already. And I simply won't be stood up. You know that new restaurant on Potrero Hill? Baxter's, I think."

"Oh yeah. It's supposed to be good."

"Okay. I'm getting reservations there for eight."

Danny agreed to the date. He had learned it was hard to head Margaret off when her mind was made up. And as he hung up, he found he was already looking forward to seeing her.

It was precisely at that moment, that the idea of making love to Margaret first seriously occurred to him. He leaned back in his chair, stunned with the thought. "Jesus, he muttered to himself, "talk about messing up the status quo." But he had to admit that a little change in his life might be a good thing. And the more he thought about it, the more attractive the idea became.

As 5:30 approached, he cleaned his desk and headed home. There, he quickly shed his clothes and fell into bed for a nap. These days, he prefaced any impending exertions, including amorous ones, with some designated rest. Waking refreshed, he took a particularly long shower and put on a dark suit he realized was a little too formal for the occasion. At 8:00 he was able to find a parking place close to the restaurant and arrived ahead of Margaret.

Nice place, he thought, as he entered the restaurant. An old warehouse with huge windows installed to command several good views. Inside, plenty of old dark wood and tile floors, with stylish tricks of green plants and neon and a pleasant dark atmosphere. An ancient maitre d' in a brand new tuxedo escorted him to his table. And very soon, the maitre d' returned with Margaret in tow. That was the thing about her. She was always punctual. And as he rose to kiss her, he remembered the other thing: she was always so damned clean. If Claudia or Kelly had a careless non-hygienic moment, Margaret never did. She tended to overdress for every occasion. Her hair was always neat and he was sure, recently dyed. And she was never without her favorite perfume, a scent that reminded him not only of Margaret, but of other women and other times he could never pinpoint, except that they were pleasant memories.

Danny complimented her on the choice of restaurant. "You like?" she asked. "Look behind you." He looked and could see out the window a spectacular view of the Financial District and the Bay Bridge, though both were muted in early evening fog. Turning back, he took Margaret's hand and squeezed it. She, in turn, fixed her eyes on him intently. "You look great, Danny," she said. "I get the idea you're on a roll."

He shrugged and managed what he hoped was a modest smile.

"You know something Danny? You're a hero of mine. You really are."

"Hero? Why do you say that?" He looked curiously at her. She was so incredibly cheerful looking. There always seemed to be a punch line lurking behind every sentence. In a way it seemed to deflate his intentions for the evening. Only in movies, he thought, do people laugh when making love.

"Well," she said, absently arranging the silverware before her, as if this were her dining room and her party, "we all have our problems. But sometimes I think you have more than your share."

"Who the hell's to say?" he said, trying not to look like he was ignoring her as he scanned the room, trying to spot a waiter.

"And yet, you don't give up," she continued. "You're like someone in a corny old book. By then he could see she was putting him on a bit. Her face agleam with a huge smile and teeth (good teeth, still her own, he was sure) glowing luminously in the darkened room. "A hero," she added once more, for emphasis.

This was more than Danny could stand. "Christ, Margaret. Pull off."

"Okay," she giggled. "You want to talk about your day?"

"Not in the least. At my age, it's pretty much going to come down to legal problems, kid problems or colon problems. Take your pick. However, to be accurate, my colon is okay for the moment."

"How are you and Stacy getting on?" she ventured, tentatively.

"So-so," he sighed. "But look, it's okay. I'll discuss it with you some time. But tonight, I just can't handle it."

Margaret shook her head. "You're telling me. I had a long-distance bout with Sandy today. That's three times this week. Last week, Sandy and Greg managed a double header. I had two long distance calls and two cries in one afternoon." Danny had an instant vision of Margaret's grown children, whom he had never met but disliked intensely from the secondhand accounts he had heard of them.

"I know. I know," he said, more than ready to change the subject. "So I'm a corny old book, huh?"

"That's right. And you, poor baby. You want a drink so bad, you're ready to tear the place up."

Danny nodded, aggressively flagged down the first tux he saw, and presently two substantial martinis stood between them. The first few swallows sent a welcome numbness through him, and in a moment, Margaret was sitting in a soft, gauzy pool of his own making, looking more than pretty. She did have good facial bones, he thought. And she was wearing a well-chosen dark blue cocktail dress that showed off what Danny always considered a pretty trim figure for her age. The trouble with clothes though, Danny reminded himself, is you can never really be sure about the body underneath until it's too late.

Dinner was excellent. First local salmon of the season, washed down by a bottle of a good Central Coast Chardonnay he had never tried before. The wine brought his spirits further up and subdued Margaret's usual effervescence to about what he thought was a proper level for romance. After they had ordered dessert Danny decided to work her into the conversational channel most likely to bring her close to a seducible range.

"Say, I almost forgot," he began, as though he really were spontaneously retrieving a remembrance. "I saw you with that Paul guy at 'The Ring' last week." She nodded and smiled.

Danny pictured the doughy face of her current boyfriend, whom he decided was definitely not good enough for her. Surely, she didn't sleep with him. "Paul looked as bored as I was," he said. "Three days of opera is a bit much. Especially Wagner."

She took a sip of her coffee and looked at him with as much seriousness as was possible with Margaret. "Maybe for you and Paul," she said finally. "I thought it was wonderful."

What the hell, Danny thought. This was a good comfort zone for Margaret. He decided to let her run with it for awhile. "Okay, tell me how you felt about it. What works for you with the Wagner?"

And so she did. Danny felt she even knew she was being patronized a bit, but she couldn't help herself. God, he thought, she really does love her opera. As much as he did his 49ers and Giants. Pleased to see this good mood, he led her from time to time with questions, but mostly she rambled on about opera as though she had never had the chance before.

By then, there was color in Margaret's cheeks, maybe from the wine. She was playful, touching him a lot, leaning across to kiss his cheek or pat his hand. They had just polished off rich desserts. The sun had fallen behind Mount Sutro, and runs of soothing jazz drifted in from the bar. The other customers whispered in their blue shadows. Maybe if there was a good time to go for it, this was it.

So, checking to see that no one was listening, he leaned close and whispered, "Margaret, let's sleep together."

"You're kidding. Like when did you have in mind?" she asked, as though waiting for the joke.

"I'm not kidding. Now. Tonight."

To his relief, she didn't laugh. Instead, for several seconds, she thought about his proposition as seriously as she had the choice of the salmon over the lamb chops. It was obvious the idea had occurred to her before. And at some considerable length and with a shrug, she said "okay, Danny." Apparently, he wouldn't even need his semi-rehearsed follow-up arguments. Without a word, he signaled for the check.

As a precaution against any change of mind on her part, Danny drove her car, leaving his parked on Potrero Hill and hoping it wouldn't be stolen before morning. Retracing his steps, he soon was driving through The Avenues to the Outer Richmond. A light, misty rain had come in with the fog, dampening the streets and wrapping a cloudy halo around each street lamp. The tires hissed on the pavement. Margaret was very quiet. And at her apartment, everything seemed different. He glanced about him at her much fussed-over plants and the antique botanical drawings on her walls as if seeing them for the first time. Her children, in photos of every age from infancy to adulthood, stared out at him accusingly from their frames.

The unfortunate thing was there was nothing else left to do. They had consumed everything one could at the restaurant, from dessert and coffee to a final cognac. Both were reformed smokers for many years, so there was no help there. So, they busied themselves turning off lights, checking the thermostat and picking up things. Generally battening down the hatches for the night, like an old married couple.

Margaret was in the bathroom for a very long time. He undressed, slid under the covers and turned on the bedside lamp, determined to see things through, whatever they were, like a man. For some time he lay there in the rosy light of the lamp, trying to fathom the meaning of an original watercolor hanging on the wall, patient in a way he knew he would never have been in his youth. And finally, she appeared, in a dark-red, bold-printed dressing gown he had seen many times on a hook on her bathroom door. When she pulled it off over her head, her familiar perfume wafted out into the room.

And it all worked out okay. Like one of the erotic dreams he sometimes had with some surprising person from his real life. One of those dreams that brought him up from sleep full of wonder and with a great shining erection. Margaret's body, he conceded, certainly outclassed his in their little show-and-tell. And all the rest he should have expected. The way she gathered him to her soft, powdered nakedness. The way she held his shoulders with her strong hands when he was inside her, in a way that was more like a trusted old friend than a lover.

Only when it was finished, did she reach over and turn out the light. As his pulse slowed in the darkness, Danny noted her quietness which he hoped wasn't a problem. He was fairly sure he had made her happy. No orgasm for her, true. But Margaret had assured him that it was okay, particularly the first time. Still, he had the tiniest fear that maybe this had altered their friendship after all. Clearing his throat first, he whispered, "you were great."

She said nothing, but gently squeezed his arm in the dark.

"Is everything okay?" he ventured, and without meaning to, added, "this doesn't change things, does it?" Why was he asking such things? Maybe he was drunk.

There was a pause in which she adjusted the covers and rolled over on her side, as though settling in. "No Danny. I'll always love you."

"That's great because . . ."

Then came her characteristic hard laugh in the darkness, that half-scared him with its suddenness. "My God," she said. "You want reassurance? Do I have a virgin here?"

This was anguishing, he thought, even though he had to laugh. What was all this chatter about? Why couldn't he just keep his mouth shut? "No, no," he protested, "this was so nice, such a turnabout from the day I've had, it's like . . . He had trouble going on.

"Like what, Danny?" she said in a kinder tone.

"Well," he began, very tentatively, "have I ever told you about the Isle of Skye?"

"No, I don't think you have," she said.

"Are you okay? Do you want me to tell about it?"

"I'm kind of sleepy. But that's all right."

"I'm sorry," Danny said, "I guess I just don't want the day to end. Go to sleep if you want. But, do you know where the Isle of Skye is?" he asked, embarrassed at his eagerness to pursue this.

"Let me think," she murmured. "Off the coast of England?"

"Actually Scotland. The Outer Hebrides."

"Is that your favorite place?" she asked, softly.

"Oh no. I don't think so. But there's something about it. I mean, it's all these somber chords. The sky is dark and kind of woolen, as though you could actually touch it. And there's so much rain and such a damp chill to the air. The fishermen get into their frail-looking boats and disappear into the fog, and you think they'll never come back."

Margaret's voice was dreamy now, humoring him, he thought, so she could escape into sleep. "You're telling me the weather's never good?"

"Oh, I'm sure it is sometimes. But I simply can't believe that. All I remember are those clouds and that chill air. And that surprising moment when the sun slashes through and throws a beam or two on the old buildings by the harbor. But somehow, in that small way, it's the sweetest sunlight in the world. Better than the tropics."

"You were there with Sadie, weren't you."

"Oh sure, but that doesn't mean anything," Danny found himself lying. "We packed in all our usual arguments. Skye isn't about Sadie. In fact, you can make it about you if you want. You're the one who changed this day."

"Don't give away your island too quickly, Danny."

He paused to think about that and lost his audience. Her breathing became deeper and then there was the slight whistle of a snore. My God, he confessed to himself, I haven't thought about the Isle of Skye in a long time. Maybe I just couldn't before. But now it seems like it's all right.

So he began to drift back into that long-ago trip to Skye, as though it were a movie that played continuously in an all-night theater. Again, he saw the little wooden hotel by the quay. The water dripping steadily from the eaves above their window. The food smells creeping up the narrow staircase from the kitchen to the little room. Later, he and Sadie strolled through the village. The shops were mostly closed for the day, but still they stopped at every window, trying to extract some meaning from the spools of thread and bolts of cloth or loaves of stale bread. In some of them, plump cats slept against the panes.

The days were so long that time of year, that even late in the evening it was still quite light. When the darkness finally did close in, they walked back to the hotel, pausing at the basement pub for one last drink. There was a table near the grate, close enough to the fire to take off the chill. Broad, ruddy faces turned to take them in. Not that many Americans on Skye. The patrons turned back to their conversations.

On a low stage near the bar, an entertainer was playing the accordion. His right hand pulled out the melodies of sassy jigs and reels. But, from the bellows, he pulled up something much deeper and sadder. Like bagpipes. When the musician smiled between numbers, you could see where a tooth was missing in front. A reminder that he was only a pub entertainer, not a priest of some profound faith. But when he began to play, he held his firm jaw up like the prow of a ship and make the customers believe again. At this point, Danny was unaware that sleep had finally found him too and what had begun as a memory actually had turned into a dream.

LINDSAY
SATURDAY

"**D**addy, Daddy!" she shrieked, charging the screen door as though she might break right through it. "Guess what, Daddy?"

She startled me, lost in my thoughts as I had been when I rang the bell. Lindsay was unpredictable, sometimes Daddy's little girl, other times a contentious brat. But her bubbling enthusiasm that morning was just what I needed. I gathered her in, and she threw her little arms around my neck.

"Daddy, I want you to see my new dress for the trip. Come on."

"What trip is that, sweetie?" I asked as she dragged me by the hand through the house toward her room. I could hear Brenda's voice from the kitchen, talking to someone on the phone.

"The trip to New York. With Mommy and Steve." She turned her head as we walked, I guess to see how I took that news. Maybe to see if I approved and if it was okay for her to go.

"I didn't know you were going to New York. I think that's great."

The dress was laid out on the white quilted spread on her bed, surrounded by a menagerie of staring stuffed animals, many of which I had bought in the last year. And the room itself was a load for me that moment, as I realized I hadn't been in it for a long time. Brenda had redecorated and rearranged most of the house, almost like a scorched earth policy to get rid of every vestige of my presence. But nothing had changed in Lindsay's room except the new stuffed animals. There was the shelf I had made, the dresser I had painted, the wallpaper I had put up. It touched me to think she had slept in this room every night since I left.

Stunned by this realization, I was startled to hear Brenda's voice. I spun around to see her leaning casually against the doorjamb, looking intently at me. "I'm sorry I didn't talk to you about the trip. I just heard about it yesterday," she said, not saying that she heard it from Steve. Just heard it, as though it had been on the radio. I stood awkwardly, looking at her. Sometimes I kissed Brenda at the door when I came to pick up Lindsay. But at this moment that seemed out-of-place.

"Listen, Mike, would you mind passing on next weekend? We'll still be in New York. Maybe you can double up your visit the week after that," she asked me, in a tone that suggested she knew she was on legal thin ice. Frankly, I loved the opportunity to be gracious.

"No, no, that's fine. I think it's great she can go. Will you take her to Central Park and all that?"

"The park, the zoo, the works. Of course."

I hugged Lindsay playfully and she squealed with delight. "How wonderful, Lindsay," I said. "You're so lucky to be going to New York." I was working this for all it was worth, as though it was me popping for the trip. And deep in my con man's heart, I also knew there was a tiny little element of delight that I could spend the next weekend with Diana for a change.

"But Daddy, you didn't look at my dress."

"I know," I said, grabbing the dress and holding it up to admire it. "Here, Sweetie," I said, "why don't you put it on and let me see how it looks?" I knew I could take this liberty, this stalling. I was clearly on the moral high ground.

"Yes, put it on for your father," Brenda said. "Mike, would you like a Coke?" she asked over her shoulder as she headed for the kitchen.

"Sure. Why not?" I answered. I could have a Coke. Plop down in one of Brenda's chairs like I owned it. Watch Lindsay pirouette through her little fashion show. I was still a good father, a considerate ex-husband.

— ·· — ·· — ·· — ·· — ·· — ·· — ·· —

Later, five Cokes swelling my bladder, I had reason to think the momentum had shifted, as I sat on a park bench and watched Lindsay going back and forth in the swing. "Here's the thing, Mike," Brenda had said, "this isn't just a little getaway trip. Steve and I are actually thinking about moving to New York. He's got a great job offer there and . . . "

"And you'd be taking Lindsay?" I blurted.

"Of course."

"You can't do that, Brenda."

"You know I can. You can't imprison us in this town."

Lindsay called to me to swing her, and I went over and began pushing her higher and higher. "You're such a good swinger, Daddy," she squealed. Lindsay was being especially pleasant this day. Dressed in expensive, kid's sized Levi's and Reeboks and pure honey coming out of her little mouth. A diplomat, like her Mommy, playing the part.

I couldn't help it. I probed just a bit while we were sipping hot chocolate in the pavilion. "Lindsay, will you miss me when you're in New York?"

"Oh yes, Daddy," she said, reaching up quickly to wrap her arms as far around my neck as they'd go. And in my ear she whispered, "and Mommy says I can write you every week."

My eyes misted over and I couldn't answer back. That would have happened anytime she was that sweet to me. But today was even more intense. I was no fool, though. I could see those letters showing up in my mail. The heavy crayon writing I could imagine being produced by her tight little fist as she leaned close to the paper on the kitchen table, her tongue going a mile a minute. Gaff hook stuff. Rip your guts right out. And the letters showing up less and less often. The annual summer visitation growing stranger each year as she went through her stages A formality, a pain in the butt to her, eventually an impossibility. "You can't disappoint your father like that," Brenda would say, secretly gleeful in her vindictive marrow.

"Oh mother! It's just too complicated," Lindsay would pout.

We had worked our way down through the park, Lindsay devouring each attraction ritualistically like the Stations of the Cross. The swings, the slide, the duck pond, the refreshment stand. Now, as the afternoon was sliding away, we walked purposefully down the perimeter path, both of us silent. Maybe I don't have to take this, I thought. I wouldn't be the first father, faced with such a monstrous scenario, to do something desperate. But what you're thinking about is a felony, I instantly thought. You could go to jail for that. And before I could stop myself, in trooped all those other considerations. I'd lose Diana. I'd lose the best job I ever had. I'd lose my Sunday foursome and poker night and . . . It killed me to see this petty flotsam gurgling out onto the stage in a play in which Lindsay was slipping out of my life.

Back at my car, I carefully packed her in, and when the door was closed, I stopped for a minute and leaned against the roof. There, I could allow the anguish to take over my face where Lindsay couldn't see me. Only time all afternoon I gave in to it. You've got to get a grip, old man, I said to myself. You're crazy to even let your mind drift in the direction you're considering.

Yes, that's right, I conceded as I walked around the car. There's absolutely nothing I can do about this.

Duty's the Boat to Gull Island

W hen Lela left the plane at Kennedy, she already
had eighteen hours of traveling behind her,
including the last leg from London to New York.
But she had slept well on the flight and decided not to stay
over but to rent a car and start driving north. It was a mistake
from the beginning. She soon found herself in the Friday exodus from New York, a bumper-to-bumper crawl through
Larmont and Greenwich and Norwalk. As the traffic thinned
somewhat through Massachusetts and Maine, she pressed
harder on the accelerator, trying to push as far as Brunswick.
There, with considerable luck, she located the last room in the
last motel in town and slept deeply, confident that she was
now very close to the island.

The next morning, much refreshed, she cut over to the
coast at Boothbay Harbor, and there, seeing the spray of gulls
against the rising sun and catching the nostalgic odor of the
fishy refuse beneath the dock, she shivered with delight. This
trip was supposed to be for Walt and Hazel, she thought to
herself, but I could use a little of this.

Lela spotted amongst the sleek schooners and cabin

cruisers moored in the slips a familiar, battered work boat she knew belonged to Harold, the old Gull Island caretaker. But when she walked up the dock toward the boat, she saw a young man aboard, loading on tools and lobster pots. He looked up at her and reading the question in her face asked, "Gull Island, ma'am?" in his thick Down East accent. She nodded, and he languidly crawled up the ladder to assist her. She then recognized him as one of Harold's sons. Just a kid when she was last there and now she guessed close to thirty, though his face, exposed to years of harsh wind, made him look much older. "Who you staying with?" the young man asked.

"The Richards."

"They'll be glad to see you," he said, in a manner that suggested everyone on the island had already discussed it and agreed unanimously.

"Aren't you Harold's son?"

"Yes ma'am," he replied. "Jason."

"Is your father still alive?"

"No ma'am."

Of course, Lela thought. No one like Harold would retire. He'd probably die while carrying firewood to a cottage or working a shrimp boat in the winter.

"Well Jason, I'm sorry," she said, her reaction genuine. Harold was a pleasant and enduring memory of all her years on the island, from her first recollections as a little girl.

Jason helped her arrange a parking space at a nearby motel and then carried her bag down to the dock. Soon they were settled in the boat and its engines kicked to life. Jason pointed the bow out to open water and then around the point into the labyrinth of islands and inlets that complicated this stretch of coast. A snow-white gull hung as though motionless off the stern, confusing the little boat for one of the tourist excursion runs where it could expect to be tossed some scraps. The wind blew Lela's hair and lashed her face with spray remarkably cold for summer in any waters but these.

As the boat reached Gull Island and cruised slowly into the leeward waters on the western side, the wind abruptly abated and the heavy chop disappeared. They glided in a strange pink morning light on a sea that appeared to be coated with sweet oil. Jason steered true to the island's little dock at what seemed to Lela collision speed. But skillfully, he quickly reversed the engines, which responded with a deep-throated groan and they eased into the pilings with just a kiss of wood on wood. The engines were shut off, leaving for the moment, a vacuum of profound silence.

Jason transferred the bag to a jeep for the trip up the hill to the Richards' cottage. Everything was the same as the day she had last seen it. The old post office, the communal well, the rustic clay tennis court where they would soon be staging the Gull Island Doubles Championship, with everybody on the island cheering from the little section of bleachers. Nothing changes, Lela thought. Maybe it's because the winters are so brutal, it's all one can do to restore the cottages and the public facilities to what they were the year before, much less make improvements.

The hard-beaten dirt path then wound through a thick woods of pine and birch and bright green fern, where shafts of sunlight broke through the branches in long, golden streams. Lela remembered these woods well, as much as her favorite outcroppings along the water's edge where she liked to sit by the hour. Surely, she would have time to spend alone at these favorite haunts. Or if Nancy was really there, as Hazel suggested, to experience them with her once more.

Walt and Hazel met her on the porch of their cottage, a very pleasant, open span of decking that commanded a spectacular view of the open sea. She could see that the antique brass telescope was still mounted proudly on the rail. Walt stepped forward and took her in his arms and pounded her back enthusiastically. "Oh, she's here, Hazel, she's here," he gushed, his voice hoarse with emotion.

Hazel was more guarded, which didn't surprise Lela. She was thin, almost painfully so and as high-strung and nervous a woman as Lela had ever known. "Oh, my dear, how we've looked forward to this," she said, offering her wrinkled cheek and as quickly pulling it away. While Walt took her bag up to her room, Hazel pulled her into the kitchen and poured her a cup of strong coffee from the blue porcelain pot on the old, gas stove. Looking around that little room, Lela lapped up all the details she had recalled perfectly half a world away. The rough, wooden shelves, the oil cloth on the kitchen table, the refrigerator door virtually covered with greeting cards and photos.

Soon they were all seated on the porch, Lela pleasantly bathed in the roar of the surf crashing just below them and the sweet smells of pine and sea.

"Let me get this straight," Walt said, leaning eagerly toward her in his straight wooden chair. Lela had been given the queen's seat, a cushioned and very comfortable porch glider. "You drove straight up here from the airport? My

God, you must be exhausted."

"I spent the night in Brunswick and caught up a little. But I guess I'm still a little jet lagged."

"Well, you'll get a nap today, I promise," Hazel interjected quickly. "I did plan a little cocktail party for tonight, if that's all right. Nancy and the Hendersons and the Fletchers. Come to think of it, you don't know the Fletchers, but they're real nice folks."

"That'll be wonderful, Hazel."

"And, oh goodness, I should have had you pick up some quinine water on the mainland. We're low, I see."

"Tell 'em to bring their own damned tonic," Walt growled. "She's our guest."

"Well, I hate to do that."

"Used to be we drank well water with our gin. Didn't hurt us a bit."

Lela shuddered, remembering this old custom, a concession to the logistical problems of living on an island. A Gull Island Cooler was what they called a gin and water. At one of the interminable cocktail parties, you were simply asked, "white or dark?" (cheap gin or whiskey with plain water).

"Tell me about Bosnia, Lela," Walt said. "You were right in the thick of it, weren't you?"

"At times."

"You ever get fired on?"

"Yes. Once we got caught in a mortar shelling. It was pretty close. A hunk of metal hit the wall right above my head."

"Oh, my stars!" Hazel screeched, her arms flung in the air and her face filled with fear.

"Settle down, old girl," Walt said. "You mean they fired right at the press? At people like you?"

"No, I don't think so. We were just in the wrong place at the wrong time."

"Was it worst than any of those other . . . ?"

"I don't know, Walt. Somalia was a little scary. El Salvador. The Gulf War, for sure. You know . . . the uncertainty."

"Was it as ugly as it looks on the news?"

"Yes. The people there have been catching it pretty good." Lela momentarily had a mental glimpse of what that meant to her, usually the sight of people's kitchen goods or a child's doll lying in the mud. Though she had seen much worse. The bodies stacked up.

"When you and Brandon were married," Hazel interjected, "I thought of him as the . . . well, 'wild one.' You were so reserved, almost shy, I guess. And here you are a war correspondent."

"Well, not in the near future. Looks like I'll be riding a desk in Washington for awhile."

"Thank God. I have to ask you, honey, I suppose you think about him a lot. We sure do."

"Of course," Lela replied. In actual fact, she sometimes forgot that Walt and Hazel were her former husband's parents.

"Viet Nam was a long time ago," Walt said, squinting out to sea. It was obvious he didn't want the conversation to get bogged down in this terrain.

"Maybe to the rest of the country it was," Hazel shot back, "they didn't lose a son. And for such a worthless . . . "

"Haz, keep just a little perspective," Walt said, patiently (Lela was grateful to her former father-in-law for echoing her unspoken thoughts). "Brandon was a West Pointer, a career officer. No matter what we may think about Viet Nam, he thought it was his job. Combat credentials are what counts to career people."

"It's true," Lela added, thinking Walt deserved some support. "The lucky heroes are three-star generals now. And the not-so-lucky are . . . "

"Dead!" Hazel finished for her, dissolving into a torrent of tears, her face buried in her hands and her whole body shaking with this sudden spasm of grief. Walt stared out to sea, Lela down at the porch decking. With no one to comfort her in her now thirty-year grief, Hazel cried herself dry and then began to tidy up with a Kleenex. "Sorry," she said, in a voice that sounded even for the first time since Lela arrived. "It must be the excitement of having you with us."

"I know," Lela said gently, patting the older woman's hand."

Walt turned back to Lela. "You know, I'm surprised you're still a single woman. My God, you're as pretty as ever."

"Well, I did marry again."

"Oh, I know," Walt replied, flatly. Lela remembered that her former in-laws had seemed more upset by her divorce from Larry than her marriage to him, the latter occurring a respectful five years after they had buried Brandon. It was as though the divorce was the true insult to their dead son's memory.

"Mine's not a good life for a married person," Lela said, finally. "I'm away almost all the time. Even when I'm in the States, the hours are long. It's just better this way."

"I guess you have a sense of duty. Just like a soldier."

Lela murmured a yes, but with no conviction. No Walt, it's not duty, she thought. This is duty, being here today. I know the difference. "No, not really. It's far more like pleasure. At least an intense satisfaction."

After they had talked for awhile on the porch, Jason chugged up in the jeep with a tub containing three lobsters he had caught in his own traps that morning. Lela was eager to help with the lunch ritual. Below the cottage was a stone oven, where Walt built a fire with discarded cedar shingles. Lela lined the bottom of an old, black iron pot with stones. The lobsters, frisky one-pounders straining their backs in an attempt to pinch their captors, followed, and then a layer of seaweed Jason had brought up from the dock area. The pot was placed on a hook over the fire and soon the air was filled with the luscious odor of cooking lobster. When they were bright red, Lela took them down to the screened-in summer house perched right on the edge of the cliff, and then she helped Hazel bring down the rest of the lunch: salad, corn-on-the-cob and cold beer.

It was a feast as rich in nostalgia as flavor for Lela. She knew how precious such a sunny day as this was, in that narrow band of August that was the best time of the year on Gull Island. She ate until she was stuffed while looking out at the brilliant burnished blue water and listening to the surf boiling on the rocks.

Then, as she had been promised, she took some time for herself. First, a long, hot shower, with full knowledge that the water had been captured in the elaborate guttering that encircled the eaves and dormers of the ancient cottage and gathered in an enormous wooden barrel. It undoubtedly contained gull droppings and whatever else might be on the roof, but it was hot and soothing nonetheless. Hardly the first time I've bathed in unpotable water, Lela thought. Some of it absolutely putrid.

Then came a nap in her designated bedroom, which was located on the ocean side, so she assumed one of them had given it up for her. The sheets were cold and salt damp, but she was so deeply fatigued, sleep claimed her quickly. If Hazel hadn't awakened her for the party, she might have slept away the night, as well as the afternoon. After she had been summoned by the rap at the door, she lay a while longer, feeling the cottage and the ocean about her. Bosnia seemed a galaxy away.

Lela would not have wanted to miss a moment of Hazel's party. The Hendersons were already there. Phyllis Henderson had been more of a mother to her when she was a girl than her own was. She was glad to be able to sit with this wonderful woman for awhile before Nancy arrived. It would have seemed a shame to have to balance both of them at once.

Then Nancy did arrive by the path. Like most of the features of the island, she had changed very little, Lela thought. Perhaps twenty pounds heavier, but still the same irony in her face, as though they both caught the humorous underside of the situation and understood each other perfectly. Lela and Nancy embraced for a long time.

"I love you," Nancy said, simply.

"Now, before you two go off and leave us," Hazel said, "I want you to meet the Fletchers, Lela," gesturing toward the couple who had just arrived on the path after Nancy. Lela shook hands with two granite-chinned New Hampshireites who seemed to reek of money. Helen Fletcher was very intense, in a way that reminded Lela of Hazel. "Oh, my God, yes. How many times have we seen you on TV? But you look the same in real life. What a thrill this is for me."

"Me too," Lela said, smiling.

"Well, how nice that you could visit Gull Island, my dear. We're just so pleased to have you here."

"But Lela is Gull Island," Nancy insisted. "Her family's been coming up here as long as mine. We grew up together, for God's sake."

Headed off on her own turf, Helen looked to Lela for confirmation, disappointment obvious in her face.

"It's true. In fact, I first met Brandon here. When we were both about eight. So, I guess I'm a native. If there's such a thing."

As soon as Lela politely could, she took Nancy's hand and headed out on the porch to a far corner where they could be alone. After lighting cigarettes, they appraised each other in the late afternoon light. "Why the hell do we do these things?" Lela asked. "I should have seen you every day of my life. Yet, I let twenty-five years slip by."

"I could say you were the big, unreachable celebrity, too far above Ol' Nancy. But I just can't. I tried to call you a couple of times, but didn't really follow through. What was so fucking important that kept me from doing it?"

"It's not too late. You're living in New York. I'm in Washington. We should try to spend some time together. At least, I've kept in touch with what you were doing over the years."

"Oh, I don't blame you, it's such an interesting story.

Kids grown, husband gone, middle-aged woman looking for truth. A unique tale in modern America."

"You forgot the undaunted part. Of course, that's what you are."

"On that undaunted note, why can't we get together this week? I'm just rattling around in that old cottage. Why don't you come over and stay with me?"

"Oh shit, I don't know. I have to walk a fine line with Walt and Hazel. They might really get their feelings hurt if I stayed somewhere else."

"How's it going here?"

"Oh, okay. We had a little scene about Brandon this morning. But then lunch and all that was fun. Just like the old days."

I'm surprised you still keep in touch like this. I mean you married again and all that. Maybe you still wear the widow's weeds, but I'd be surprised to hear that."

"You know me pretty well. But it's a little worse than you think."

"How do you mean?"

"Well, every family has its secrets. One of ours was that Brandon's going off to war interrupted our imminent divorce plans."

"Oh, I see."

"In fact, to be honest, I was already seeing Larry while Brandon was over there. And I'm sure he was screwing everything that walked."

"That bad, huh?"

"Oh God, we despised each other. It wasn't just a difference of opinion. That's why I'm pretty sure of what he was doing during R&R, because that's exactly what he was doing here. Brandon just couldn't get enough of women. Other than his wife."

"I'd heard that."

"I'm sure you did. But then he had to go and get himself killed. And that muddied things up a bit. So I sort of got the grieving widow role for the rest of my life."

"There's a statute of limitations on that, you know. You have no real obligation to your old in-laws anymore."

"Yeah, but there's another family secret, Nancy. After Brandon died, I started getting checks from Walt's Bank. Walt said it was some kind of trust fund pledged to Brandon but not part of the estate. According to the terms, as long as I was unmarried, I'd receive the interest on it. It was a lot of money, the kind of money that makes you not ask questions. But eventually, I did do some snooping around and discovered the money was just coming right out of Walt's account. A gift. I think I actually married Larry for just two reasons. It stopped the payments without having to make a scene over it. And, I'm ashamed to say it, Larry, or at least his money, made it possible for me to do without that stipend from Walt."

"Well, honey, we do what we have to. But Larry just didn't work out?"

"Not for a minute. He was essentially cut out of the same cloth as Brandon. In time, it didn't matter. I made plenty of money on my own by then. And I was out of the country most of the time."

"What about other men? Do you ever think about finding someone?"

"No. I have plenty of friends, men and women. I have

my work, which I love. Sometimes, I'll take a fling with someone, but less of that all the time. It just doesn't seem as important anymore."

"But Lela, why do you stay anchored to Walt and Hazel? Even with their generosity, there has to be a limit?"

"Family. Let's face it, my folks are dead. I have no brothers or sisters. I'm away almost all of the time, so no obligation's going to be too much of a problem. What's it cost me to write them every month or so and visit them once in awhile? To pretend things are what they want them to be? It's nice to have some family, Nancy. Just like it's nice to have old friends."

Nancy considered this for a moment and then said, "God what a great place this was. I mean when we were growing up."

"I know. I was thinking today about all the things we used to do. What a rag-tag gang of brats we were. And the trouble we got into."

"Nobody seemed to give a damn then, Lela. Jesus, we used to play all those dangerous games out on the rocks. How come nobody ever got killed?"

"And when we got older we were always slipping off to smoke a joint or drink our folks' booze."

"I got laid the first time on this island."

"Who the hell didn't? But God, Nancy, think of all the people we knew. All those generations . . . "

"A patriarch or a matriarch in every cottage, wouldn't you say? Gathering their families around them, coming back every summer like it was a pilgrimage. All those people, and a lot of them dead now."

"I remember your grandmother so well, handing out cookies to us at her kitchen door."

"And your mom, Lela. I always thought she was a better woman than you did."

"She was. I know that now. She was actually a better woman than *me*. It takes a long time to figure out things like that."

Lela put out her cigarette on the concrete step and they both fell silent for a moment as they stared out at the water, very still and luminous in the fading light. Lela thought about all the times she and Nancy had stood together like this at dusk, as little girls or as teenagers, talking quietly, trying to stall the need to be separated from each other and to go home to dinner or to bed. A voice from inside the cottage suddenly made them both turn their heads toward the windows. It was Hazel's voice echoing through the rooms, loud and shrill.

"Lela? Where's Lela? Anyone know where those two went?"

TRIPLES

Like most people who live in tourist towns, Max had a favorite time of year, that sliver of late November when the visitors have all gone home and the weather is still almost perfect. As he crossed Cabrillo Boulevard on his way to meet Sid for lunch, he was pleased to see that the public pier and the normally busy commercial area were almost empty. A determined morning breeze, cooler than usual, swept scrap paper before it and licked up whitecaps on the dark blue water. Even the sea gulls seemed to join in the spirit as they turned into the wind and hovered with their wings motionless.

Max had to question his feelings about the annual exodus of the tourists. As an owner of two McDonald's Restaurants in Santa Barbara, the diminished off-season traffic certainly cut deeply into his receipts. He could only shrug and think that, after all, maybe there was more to life than making money. He and Sid had certainly agreed on that long ago. Max giving up an imposing corporate career at McDonald's' in return for his two locations. And Sid sacrificing a Vice Presidency with Hilton for the Dunes Motor Lodge that stood in a row of similarly undistinguished stucco motels on the landward side of Cabrillo.

That day, the only occupant of the Dunes's tiny lobby was a portly, red-faced salesman, sipping his complimentary coffee from a plastic cup and squinting at the local sports page. At the desk was Hilda, the cashier, her pale face wrinkled and rouged beneath orange-rinsed frizzy-hair, squinting at Max through rhinestone glasses anchored with little gold chains, and Charles, the desk clerk, so perpetually exasperated, it appeared at any moment he would fly apart. They sat, as usual, side by side, passing judgments like local magistrates on the guests as they arrived or checked-out. Charles, rolling his eyes and flapping his hands in frustration, was quick to fill Max in on that day's problems. "Max . . . he's even worse than ever," he bleated, "it's his birthday, he says, for Christ's sake."

As if to punctuate the point, a voice came booming from behind the door of the manager's private office. "Listen, you asshole, you run your fucking business and I'll run mine!" the voice roared to what one assumed was a helpless party on the other end of the phone line. "My God, what a mouth," said Hilda, absently, apparently accustomed to her boss's frequent scenes. From the other room, there was the abrupt slam of the receiver, a flurry of shuffling and bumping, then the door was flung open violently. Out of it emerged Sid, as placid as though he had just ended a nap instead of a tirade. Had not the three people at the desk known him well, they might have craned their heads to see past him and discover who had really staged the tantrum they had just heard.

"Hey Max, boy," Sid said, brightly. "You buying me

lunch? It's my . . . "

"Birth-day," Charles finished for him, again rolling his eyes with impatience.

"Right," Sid said, with finality, hitching up his tie and buttoning his sport coat. He produced a comb and ran it through his slicked dark hair which Max was sure was dyed. He was all a kind of perpetual motion, surprisingly quick for a heavy man. Almost, but not quite, effeminate.

"Tourist season's over, Sid," Max offered. "We can get any table we want on the deck at the Clam Box."

"Naw, let's go to the Mirage."

"But God, Sid. It's a gorgeous day," Max protested.

"No arguments, pal," Sid said, shutting him off. "It's my birthday. So, the Mirage it is."

"Get him out of here, Max," Charles pleaded, flipping his hand in dismissal.

"Take your time, boss," Hilda added. "Don't worry about us."

Already, Sid was walking so rapidly through the lobby, Max had to step quickly to catch up. "Sounds like they hate to see you go, Sid," he offered, cheerily.

"Morons, Max. Don't know a great man when they see one. Especially on his birthday."

"Hey, but look. With the tourists gone, why don't we do the Clam Box?"

"You can't be stopped," Sid sighed. "Okay, I'll buy the first round. But it's got to be the Mirage."

Always attuned to a bargain, Max instantly ceased all argument and walked obediently up the street beside his friend. "Fine thing," Sid muttered. "Have to bribe people to humor me on my birthday."

"It's the least you can do," Max said. "By the way, did you have time to look at the line this morning?"

"This time of year I've got lots of time. Do you understand the line this week? New York seven over Frisco? The Packers over the Vikings? Are they fucking crazy?"

"The public makes the line, Sid. They're dumb asses."

"I'll say. Well, we'll go over it in a minute. How you doing, pal?" He turned and looked sideways at his friend as though suddenly his health was in serious question."

"Never better," Max answered, a little hesitantly.

Sometimes when Sid looked at him like that or made tentative inquiries about how he felt, Max could scarcely wait to get to a mirror and see if there were some telltale signs that might signal catastrophic illness. All he would see was the discouraging vision of a bald-headed gnome staring back at him. His doctor assured him, as he appeared in his office at least every other month or so with some complaint, that he was sound as a dollar.

But in his heart, he suspected that Sid's concerns were a diversion from his own, more obvious ailments. There had been a time, when Sid had shared his fears. He had described to Max, step by step, all the tests, the appointments with specialists and the outpatient procedures. It seemed to Max a scary trail that seemed to be leading toward something huge and shadowy. But the something never materialized in their conversations, and Sid finally ceased to discuss his health altogether. Max was certain it was not because the news was good. He also was sure the specialists wouldn't approve of Sid's drinking, smoking and continued overweight.

So, he began to think of Sid's friendship as something on loan. It was a great sadness to him, because no one else filled all the niches the way Sid did. Only Sid bridged the span from where they both had once been to the present. Their lunches, their occasional rounds of golf, had, to Max, become a kind of framework that held up much of what was happening to him. It troubled him greatly to think of a long life ahead without Sid. Sometimes, he even thought about discussing it with Elaine.

But that didn't seem to work. He would sit on the glassed-in porch with his wife, the curtains tight against the hot afternoon sun, as they sipped their silent cocktails that preceded their silent dinner. He had trouble not staring at her. Elaine was still beautiful, he decided. Too pretty to be married to a gnome. But he could remember when she was young as well as beautiful. His young second wife, the scandal of their friends. It seemed incredible that the subtle veil of age would ever settle over her delicate little profile. Elaine would never "lose it" the way his first wife Betty did, but it still shocked him to see any sign of her mortality. And, in the face of this confusion, he could never talk to her about Sid. Certainly, he couldn't throw himself into her arms, like he sometimes had with Betty when he was young and scared, and wail against everything that was happening.

So, he would finish his dinner, and numbly sit before the TV for a couple of hours. Finally exhausted, he would make his excuses and retire to bed, wishing only to pull sleep in over the troubled landscape of his thoughts. Then, in the healing light of morning, he would call Sid on the phone to make sure everything was all right and lunch was still on.

The Mirage was located off a side street several blocks back from the beach. At the doorway, Max found he was regretting giving-in on the choice of lunch spots. Along the Marina, all those fish houses with their outdoor tables would be washed in sunshine and salt breezes, and they could sip their drinks looking out at the water. In many ways, Max had never stopped thinking like a tourist. The Mirage, on the other hand, exuded a sour beery smell out to the street, and as they stepped out of the sunshine, the interior seemed as gloomy as a tomb. But Sid was oblivious to the contrast and was still buoyant. He pushed directly in, as though he owned the place, and directed Max to join him at the corner of the bar, so that they were half facing each other. Big Nell, the bartender, sauntered over. "The usual, gents?"

"Yeah," said Sid, without even asking his companion. "And thanks for the openers, Nell, the howdy-dos, the niceties . . . you miserable slut."

"No trouble at all, shithead," Nell said, as she reached for the glasses. "All part of the service." She threw ice cubes brusquely into two lowball glasses, slapped them on the bar with a clang, and raising the bottle of Johnny Walker Black, poured with a liberal hand that showed the insults were obviously a put-on.

Max stared at this drink, feeling a little awkward. Even though he had listened to Sid and Nell's playful banter for years, he always had this instinctive desire to be extra nice to her when he was with Sid. "Can you get some lunch for us at the bar?" he asked, quietly. "I mean, is it too crowded?"

"Too crowded?" Nell said. "Look around and tell me if you see any customers."

Max took a couple of sips and felt the whiskey burning all the way down. Elaine had been trying to get him to put some water in his drinks, but he still had trouble doing it. The fact that the drink had been ordered for him slightly eased his conscience on that score. Sid took a big swig, lit a cigarette, and put the pack and lighter on the bar as though establishing turf.

"We just couldn't go to some outdoor place, where the wind would take the smoke out of my face, could we?" Max taunted him.

"Told you, it's my birthday. Let's see your picks," he added, holding a plump hand out impatiently. Max took out his wallet and pulled a clipping from that morning's sports section where he had scribbled his choices. Sid tilted his chin so he could look at the paper through his tiny, half-moon reading glasses. "Oh ho," he exclaimed, pursing his lips and tapping his cigarette on the edge of the ashtray. "You're going with Phoenix over Miami?"

"Well God, Sid. Look at that spread. Nine points, are you kidding? And Miami's got three guys out of the defense this week."

"Interesting," Sid mumbled and continued down the weekend schedule of games. Though he wasn't asked, Max offered an insight into his reasons for each pick, feeling just a touch of pride that he was so much on top of the football scene. Sid was about the only one he knew he could show off to on the subject. Finally, Sid finished and folded the little slip of paper. "Want me to call this in for you?" he asked.

"Sure, if you would," Max said. He peeled five twenty-dollar bills from his wallet and put it on the bar. "I feel confident this week."

Nell came down the bar and refilled their drinks. She stood for awhile, leaning against the rack of bottles with her arms crossed, staring out the door. Her eyes were wide-open, so Max could see the sunny street outside reflected perfectly in them. Max had always thought Nell was pretty and liked to look at her, especially when she was quiet and thoughtful like this and wasn't heaving insults and profanity. Sid, however, wasn't quite as respectful of her repose.

"Hey, you stupid broad, how 'bout a menu?"

Nell turned slowly and threw him a glance of total contempt, but somehow her wistful mood wouldn't break to compose a retort. She pulled two stained menus from behind the cash register and tossed them on the bar.

"Any specials, Nell?" Max asked.

"Nothing special. And I wouldn't touch that meat loaf with Sid's dick."

The menus stayed on the counter, and when Nell came around again, Sid ordered another round. Max started to raise his hand to deal himself out, but then sighed and put it down. It wasn't often they had more than two. It was a pivotal choice, because he knew, past that point, he would do nothing more that afternoon. And would probably be a little foggy and headachy the rest of the day. Oh, who cares, he thought. We're celebrating the end of the season anyway.

"So what's going on with you, Sid?" he asked.

"Well, funny you should ask. I been thinking about . . . Chicago."

"What about Chicago? You don't mean you wish you were in Chicago?"

"That's right, I've been thinking that I kind of wish I

was in Chicago. Is that fucking crazy or what?"

"Jesus, I don't know. Do you have any family in Chicago . . . or friends, anymore?"

"Not a one. Course, who do I have out here? Except you."

"Sid, this is better than Chicago. You know that."

"I don't know about that. The Cubs ain't here. The ribs, the steaks, . . . the little blues clubs on Rush Street . . . "

"The blues clubs moved to Lincoln Park."

"Well, whatever. And, oh yeah, the Hancock Building, with all those little gals running around in those big quilted coats. Remember?"

"Sid, the Hancock's not even the tallest any more. There's the Sears Tower."

"Fuck it. I still miss all that stuff."

"How about the ocean . . . the weather?"

"They got the lake. And I'm indoors most of the time anyway. Like right now."

"I don't know what to say," Max admitted, feeling just a little fearful from the drift of this conversation. "You'd just pack up and go back to Chicago?"

"Well, maybe I'd go stay there for awhile and see what I thought. You know, I get these scenes in my mind. You remember how it was when it started to get dark real early in the winter and the street lights would come on along Lake Shore Drive? You know, they had those old-fashioned globes on the poles. Wasn't that great looking?"

"Yeah it was. But I don't remember much else good about the winter."

"And I was thinking about this one time. I went into a little Greek bakery up near Clark Street. There was this cute little girl in front of me, buying some sweet rolls. So, I kind of struck up a conversation with her. Then we had a cup of coffee together. They had a couple of tables, you see. And then, damned if we didn't go over to her place. She had a flat off Clark or somewhere."

"Listen pal, that was a long time ago. You were younger then. You don't think about going back and seriously chasing pussy like that?"

"Oh, I know that. But let me tell you about her. She didn't seem to have much heat in her place. And it really was a pit. Then she took off her clothes, and she was all kind of shivery and goosebumpy and kind of skinny and pitiful looking. I wasn't sure then I wanted to do it. But when I put it in, she was real warm inside, surprisingly so. And good, too. So, afterwards we ate the pastries she had bought, right out of the sack, while we're lying around in her bed. And then we did it again. In fact, two more times."

"That was then, Sid. This is now. You couldn't do a triple now if your life depended on it."

"I know. I know. What the hell though, let's drink to those triples anyway," he said, tossing back the dregs in his glass.

Max got up to go to the men's room and noticed that he was getting substantially drunk. When he came back, there were two fresh drinks on the bar. He could already see Elaine's anger when he came home smashed. But somehow, it seemed the damage was already done.

Sometimes, when they were together like this, Max considered how amazing it was that their lives were so entwined that both had taken such radical career leaps.

Certainly, they had talked about it long enough. It seemed there were few times when the sun went down in those days, that they weren't in some watering hole off Michigan Avenue, ties undone, working on their Scotches and bitching about how life was tossing them about. Of course it had to be Sid making the first move. And, he just had to follow suit. There was a lot of confusion then. They both had divorces. And when all the smoke had cleared, they were knocking back their drinks in West Coast bars instead of Chicago. Neither one sure how it had happened and really not sure why. Max sometimes saw he and Sid as the sole inhabitants of some kind of island that grew smaller all the time, the waves lapping closer and closer to their feet.

"Say, pal," Sid said, "you ever have regrets about Chicago?"

"Not about leaving it," Max replied.

"No? Well, what about?"

"Regrets," Max mused. "Well, the other day I was thinking about this Cindy."

"Who's Cindy?"

"She was Betty's best friend."

"Betty, your first wife? I don't remember a Cindy."

"No, I guess you wouldn't. She lived in Detroit. But she came to visit in Chicago a time or two when Betty and I were first married."

"So, what was the regret?" Sid asked.

Max gathered himself, surprisingly grateful to be telling this story to Sid. "Well, one time, we were having lunch, the three of us. I liked Cindy okay, you understand. I could see that she was a bit of a bitch and not my type, but I liked her anyway. Well, Betty had to go back to work, so Cindy and I were finishing our coffee. And I remember something happened. Like she said something kind of interesting just as we were getting ready to leave. So, I reached my hand out to pat hers across the table. You know how people do that. But, all of a sudden, she takes my hand in both of hers and starts kissing it and rubbing it against her cheek."

"Oh, shit. And Betty's best friend, huh."

"Yeah. So, we go out to the parking garage so I can drive her back to her hotel. Suddenly we're in my car, swapping spit and carrying on. I got inside her blouse and I'm playing with her tits. I even say, do you feel like going to bed? And she says yes she does."

"So, you did?" Sid asked.

"Nope," Max replied, shifting uncomfortably on the bar stool.

"You're shitting me."

"No. And I can't really tell you why. I guess it was because Betty and I had just gotten married and I wasn't really prepared to cheat on her. Cindy had kind of surprised me. "

"Yeah I know," Sid conceded. "It's like a damned bank loan. The only way you can get it is to prove you don't need it."

"Maybe so. It wasn't like I told her no. In fact, I thought we were going to do it at some point. But I could tell the rest of the time I knew Cindy she thought I was crazy."

"So, you never boffed her?"

"That's right," Max replied. "I tried later. But you don't do something like that to a woman. She was ready that particular day. I rebuffed her. That was that."

"Damn."

"Yeah. I thought about all that the other day, and I found myself cringing. I'm still embarrassed after twenty years. "

"Well hell, Max. That shit's kind of tough, but, I mean it's not like Greek tragedy or something. I mean, aren't divorces and all that tougher?"

"I don't think so. When you love a woman, and you spend a lot of time together, you run the course with it. You find where it works and where it doesn't. And, a lot of times, it doesn't work at all, and that's okay too, I guess. So, most of the regrets come down to the things you didn't do. Not just in love, but everything."

"The moments not seized," Sid sighed.

"Exactly. So you see why it's so painful."

"Sure I do. But it all points out what I always said about you, Max. You are one dumb fuck."

Max swung a playful punch at his friend which Sid ducked expertly and laughed aloud. Max shook his head, clearing the Cindy story from his mind, and turned in his seat and followed Nell with his eyes as she walked out to the street. She paused out there on the sidewalk, took a drag on her cigarette and slowly looked first one direction up the street and then the other. As if to find some customers she could pull into the bar.

The light outside seemed very strange and fuzzy to Max. He suddenly recalled that daylight savings time had just ended, and the sun would be setting at five o'clock or so. It would be beautiful along the beach that evening. The deep orange sunset painting the sand, the breakwater and the sails of the boats as they eased into the channel at the marina. If they had gone to the Clam Box, as he wanted, they could be watching it all.

That was what the West Coast was about to Max, that strange evening sun that always made him think of Wes Montgomery's guitar that they used to hear, ironically enough, in clubs back in Chicago. A pervasive light like that would stop at nothing. It would even sneak through the tinted windows of the lounges along Cabrillo, staining the keyboards where piano players made silky music. There would be just a few tourists left, fresh from their naps and squeaky clean from the spas, listening to the music. "Welcome to the Club California, ladies and gentlemen. I'll be playing for you until eleven o'clock." Max was so locked to the vision that he could sense its cleansing aura, even in the Mirage. Nell flipped her cigarette butt into the street and strolled back inside. When she slipped behind the bar again, Sid ordered another round.

FOLLOWING SOCRATES

Richardson could tell the two young graduate students from the cruise ship were impressed with him. They stared in admiration when he greeted the cab driver in Greek and then told him exactly where they should be dropped off at the edge of the Plaka. "Richie," the tiny blonde called Felicia gushed at him, "you really do know Athens."

"I told you," Nicole, the tall dark-haired one insisted. "Richie's a real man of the world." Richardson blushed and tried on his warmest, bon vivant smile. This was a wonderful way, he thought, to spend the few hours they would be in Athens. Such beautiful girls. And smart, too. The night before, they had talked for hours over brandy and coffee. They knew their classical architecture, all right. But he knew he had outflanked them on the being there, on seeing first-hand the wonders of the Peloponnese, Ephesus, and Crete. They marveled at his experience and seemed eager to accompany him on his visit to the Acropolis.

He had, for this occasion, worn his seersucker suit with a bright orange silk shirt and a wide-brimmed straw plantation hat. Later on, it might be a bit warm for a suit, but he had decided it was worth it. If there was a flaw in the plan, it was that the narrow, cobblestone streets of the Plaka could not be driven in a cab. One had to be let out at some point to walk, and even his cane and the occasional assistance of his companions weren't enough. He shuffled along slowly and painfully in the heat, and if it weren't for the frequent stops the two women made at the various shops along the way, Richardson doubted he could have made it. But, his spirits rose when they finally reached the great confluence of open cafes at the heart of the ancient city. There, at a comfortable table beneath the trees, he was able to regain his strength, and as he ordered wine and lunch for them, he became buoyant and expansive again.

"Richie," Nicole inquired, leaning close to him and tucking her hand in the crook of his arm, "is the Parthenon really all it's cracked up to be?"

"That and more, my dear. If anything, the underrated wonder of the world. Sad a shape as she's in, I think she's still more beautiful than anything standing today. But just think, when she was dedicated, Socrates himself attended the ceremonies."

"No kidding?" Felicia asked, her beautiful blue eyes wide with wonder. "So this is very special to you."

"You have no idea," Richardson replied. "I think each time I've been up there, my first thought is 'I wonder how many more times before I die.'" The first trip, I guess I was nearly your age. And this time . . . oh, I don't know . . . maybe it's my twelfth or so. And yet, I'm already feeling greedy. I want to know it won't be the last."

"Well it won't," said Felicia, leaning over the table to

clutch his hand. As she did, the front of her light cotton blouse opened up like a flower to Richardson and he could see her firm, tanned breasts bursting over the lace. Confident that his gaping eyes were secure behind his sunglasses, he happily stared at length.

"And you know, don't you, I have never been in such charming company," he beamed and then fell silent a moment, trying to remember if that literally was true. A brief review of wives, lovers and traveling companions flashed through his mind. But none better than these two.

Nicole was now looking upward though a space in the tree limbs, shielding her eyes from the sun, toward the ruins above them. "It looks so high up there. Will you be able to handle the climb? Is there an elevator?"

"Oh my no, my dear. I think the old Greeks figured if you couldn't climb it, you were past the joys of seeing it. But I think I'll be okay. If I can just take it slow."

But Richardson was over-confident. There were at least twice as many steps as he remembered. And he had somehow forgotten that it doesn't pay to let the summer sun rise very high before you climb. He was soon exhausted and even a little light-headed. He finally flopped down on a stone bench, defeated. "Go on," he wheezed, barely able to get his breath. Felicia and Nicole protested at length. They wouldn't go on without him. No, he insisted, they shouldn't miss such a sight. Forcefully, he waved them away.

But once they had disappeared around a turn in the stone stairway, he was sorry he had been so gracious. They should have been more considerate, he brooded. To just leave him alone like this. What if he had some real trouble, like with his heart. As what seemed like an interminable time went by, his agitation grew until he was quite angry. He had walked this way so many times, spent so many hours standing trans-fixed at the top, he was well aware at how long the visit could take. He had nothing to read and no one to talk to. He could only watch the steady procession of eager tourists, of every possible nationality, as they moved past him. A glance at his watch showed they had been gone only thirty-five minutes. It could be another hour more.

Then, to his surprise, he saw their smiles appear in the throng of people coming down the stairs. He was so totally shocked, he didn't know whether to be angry or relieved. "I never expected you back so . . . " he stammered. Then he saw that they weren't alone. Eagerly, Nicole pushed two large young men toward him. Germans he guessed, before he even heard the accents in their greetings.

"Well, what are you waiting for?" Felicia insisted. Without a word, the two descended on him and abruptly he was lifted up into the air. At last secure on the shoulders of one of the young men, he was transported right up the steps, swaying crazily like an elephant ride he had once taken in India. His first reaction was outrage, and he was tempted to turn his cane loose on these impertinent boys. Seeing the set of his jaw, Nicole reached up, took his hand gently and said, "Richie, don't you be mad. This is the only way up. We just had to do it."

At first, he considered only the embarrassment, the humiliation. But now, he could see in the surprised faces in the crowds coming down, what looked more like admiration, even envy. He began to picture himself as a revered sultan, riding on the shoulders of his man-servants, while his harem girls held his hands, stroked his legs and shouted encouragement to him. Up, up they went (he could not believe the strength of his mount) under the shade of the olive trees and through the labyrinth of crumbled walls.

At last, they broke into the sunshine on the top of the Acropolis. There it was again: the snow-white marble skeleton of the Parthenon against the blue sky, the Porch of the Goddesses, the sleepy streets of the Plaka and the modern city all laid out beneath them. "Be careful," he started to say, remembering how slippery the marble flooring could be, polished as it was by the feet of twenty-five centuries of tourists. But the German boy had been there before, and he was watching himself. Carefully, almost reverently, he lowered Richardson to the ground, to the hugs and kisses of the young women.

Near them was a small group of schoolchildren, herded closely together by adult leaders, their excited, high-pitched voices, obviously British, making a fearful row. But two voices came isolated to his ears from the group. "Who the hell is that?" said one.

"I don't know. He must be a bloody king or something."

Yes, that's it, Richardson thought, his heart pounding with happiness. I am, by God, a bloody king.

FIREFLIES

Whistle while you work.
Hitler is a jerk.
Mussolini pulled his weenie.
Now it doesn't work.

While Danny and his friends sang this refrain at the top of their lungs on the sidewalks, their fathers went off to jobs in the defense plants of Chicago and Gary, and their mothers rolled bandages for the Red Cross. Very few of Danny's friends' fathers actually went to the big war. They were borderline, a little too old or had too many children. So they contented themselves with the sacrifices and effort on the home front. Even Danny had hauled his old metal and rubber toys in his wagon to the scrap drives, supposedly to be melted into howitzers and jeep tires.

Many people admitted later that the war years were the best times of their lives. There was this great sense of belonging not found in the routines of peacetime. In fact, despite all the hardships people faced, the national suicide rate actually plummeted. That's why it was so incredible to Danny that his father chose to take his life in 1944 while employed in the war effort and at a time when the Allies apparently had the thing won. From the first moment he was aware that his father had committed suicide, he was determined to know the cause.

It wasn't an easy task. His mother died in 1952, while Danny was still young, before he found the opportunity to talk to her in depth and candor about his father. In his conversations, over the years, with surviving relatives and friends of his parents, no one knew or was willing to disclose any clues to his father's motives. Danny's parents were simple people who kept no diaries and apparently wrote few letters.

But still, there were the odds and ends that families tend to accumulate, mostly collected in trunks and cardboard boxes in the attic of his mother's home. Danny enlisted the help of his younger sister, Elise, who shared a little of his curiosity, in exploring this meager record. Before their mother's estate was probated and the two of them were packed off to an aunt's house where they would live until they were adults, they spent two long days in the attic. Sifting through the papers and effects of several generations, looking for anything that might offer an explanation for their father's death. For the rest of Danny's life, whenever he caught that distinctive odor that prevails in attics and other enclosed, dry places, he instantly thought of those two days when he and Elise explored the family effects in the attic. He would clearly see her kneeling beside him on the rough boards as an October sun poured through the casement window and illuminated great curtains of accumulated dust.

He would remember the excitement as they explored box after box of bills and postcards and ticket stubs and thank-you notes. Photos of forgotten relatives at picnics and reunions. The women sourly prim in stiff, white blouses and long skirts. The men, mugging for the camera in celluloid collars and straw boaters. They moved slowly, full of wonder, through the photo albums that documented their own young lives, crammed so full of snapshots that many had broken the weak bonds of the dry mucilage and lay loose in the album pages. As supporting players, his parents appeared here and there in those recorded dramas, their smiling faces revealing that strange awareness of their own mortality people always imagine in photographs of the dead.

Ultimately, the attic was as tight-lipped as the friends and relatives had been. Even the partnership with Elise proved short-lived. Although they remained close over the years, in time she became reluctant to discuss their father's suicide with him.

Danny, at last, was left with the only remaining records that could be studied, his own memories. They were feeble recollections indeed since he had been only six years old when his father died, and they seemed to come in two separate pieces. First there was the funeral itself, with the sight of his father lying still in the casket, the gathered friends and relatives and the food that was brought in by neighbors. All of this was quite vivid in his memory. The other remembrance was their summer vacation at the lake that had been interrupted by the suicide. That memory lay in the vault clear and distinct and real and quite separated in his head from the death. There, he felt, must lie the clues.

So, Danny began a process that would last all his life, a mental exercise of exploring that distant summer. He took the shreds and pieces of the lake vacation and looked at them from many directions, turning them in the light, tempering them in his own experience as he first grew up and then grew older. Always looking for another angle, another way of understanding. Waiting patiently for that rare occurrence when a whole new shred would somehow emerge from his brain, like a dead body that pops up from a river bottom.

It was an easy kind of research. From time to time, when he had the time alone, he would simply close his eyes and summon up his memories of the summer at the lake. Always expectant that this time the gauzy soft colors of that long-ago world would this time rearrange and there it would be. "The reason I killed myself was this . . . "

Once again, as it almost always was at the beginning, Danny's father exclaimed excitedly, "Look, there she is!" They all snapped to attention. His mother craned forward in the front seat, eager, as always, to seem appreciative. Danny, of course, was restless in the back seat from the long ride and uncoiled like a spring and bounced spastically against the door. Elise, who had been pouting over some perceived injury from her brother, sat up quickly, her eyes wide. Even Amanda, their ancient cat, stretched and yawned and approached a begrudged animation. They all looked out expectantly at that same curve in the road, where the seemingly endless corn fields parted like a curtain to reveal the expanse of water.

The lake unfolded in a breath, ringed with row on row of brightly-painted cottages, white and yellow, red and blue. Each cottage accented with its identically-painted outhouse. Then, as now, a vacation was a step back from the realities of the present and people were pleased to read again by kerosene lamps, put blocks of ice in their wooden ice boxes and relieve themselves on toilets that couldn't be flushed. That first view of the lake still popped through in his mind with crystal clarity even though no such sight remained on the planet.

Many years later, Danny revisited that lake and had trouble recognizing it as the same place. Not only were there real changes like the absence of outhouses and ice wagons, but there were changes in his perceptions too. By that time, he had seen Tahoe and Como, as well as real windswept oceans, and a muddy lake gouged from a flat Midwestern plain no longer offered the magic he had once felt. Still, nothing in his life could rival that moment when a certain turn in the road cued his father to alert the family and they all saw the water before them.

"Let's stop now," Danny's father said, "before we're too tired." His practicality always overcame his family's grumbling shortsightedness. And he pulled into a country gas station to fill up the old Plymouth. The gas station had glass pumps where Danny could see the red gasoline inside. Even then, that was a rustic novelty to city dwellers. After the car was gassed up and the windshield wiped clean, they went into a little grocery, scrambling up concrete steps so high the children had to be assisted in climbing them, through a slam-bang screen door bedecked with a rusted metal sign advertising root beer. Such a wondrous smell burst forth from that dark, little room crammed full of shelves and counters, an odor still sweet in Danny's mind, of wax and rot and old wood and festering produce. The country grocer welcomed them in with red-faced joy, wiping his hands expectantly on a white apron.

Quickly they filled up two big cardboard cartons with groceries of strange regional brand names and cartons of Dr. Pepper and hamburger wrapped in white paper tied with twine. Danny's father, smiling and winking at his son, carried out the boxes on his shoulders. Then, the grocer's boy went out back with the tongs and brought back a steaming block of ice, clear and blue all the way through, carrying it with effort on his back, and put it on a burlap bag in the backseat floor where Elise and Danny could worry with it and rub against its shocking cold surface with delighted shrieks and howls.

Then, by narrow streets and bumpy lanes, they arrived at last at the cottage, which was at the end of the lake's developed area, where a meadow ran up from the water's edge to the cornfields above. The owner had already set the cottage in order, rolled out the mattresses on the springs to take the air and swept the step and porch clean. An American flag flapped from the eaves over the porch and with every window propped open, the curtains waved crazily in all the rooms. Danny and Elise ran through the cottage in perpetual excitement while the block of ice was wrestled into the ice box, the groceries put away and the clothes placed carefully in closets secured only by muslin curtains hung on wooden rods.

They were the first to arrive. The Johnson's were there within the hour with their two sons, to be shyly ignored at first and later accepted as blood brothers. There was even a dog for Amanda to hiss at. Another two couples moved into the cottage next door, and the four families began the process of linking together. The adults bustled about in that resonant wooden interior, putting away more things and speaking in loud voices and laughing. Someone broke out a bottle of low quality wartime gin, and soon the voices were even louder. The men stripped to their undershirts, and sprawled on the kitchen chairs, puffing on their Lucky Strikes and wartime substitute Marvels cigarettes. As darkness closed in, they clumsily and drunkenly fumbled with the kerosene lamps, laughing at each other's ineptitude. But finally, someone managed to light the wicks and make the mantles glow correctly. The lamplight blazed orange across the naked rafters.

Danny revisited that day and that night with the careful scrutiny of a stamp collector lifting his materials with tweezers and soberly scanning them with the magnifying glass. What could there have been in the folds of that bright afternoon ("Look, there she is!") and the gin-fired evening to follow? In truth, that one day was the only glimpse of all the adults about him that remained to Danny. So, he had to make do with it as a specimen. Was there a rival, he often pondered. Was his mother somehow involved with Mr. Johnson or one of the two men next door? Was his father in love with one of the women? Was there some hostile intimidation in the air that night that might have filled his father with lethal levels of self-doubt? Or was that very gaiety, as he later would learn in his own life, the stuff of despair? The hollow New Year's Eve toast and the light bubbling wine that turns flat and sticky when daylight appears.

He remembered, though in fact he was not that sure it was even the same night, trying to sleep under the bare, unfamiliar studs and lathing of his loft bedroom. Finally, drawn by the distant, hypnotic murmur of talk and laughter below, he crept down the scary wooden steps, where shadows danced on the boards. Through a gap in the railing, he silently observed the party below. In the haze of smoke, he saw a back view of his father at the kitchen table, still in his undershirt, bent over a poker hand. He could see the muscles of his back and shoulders working and his ears sticking out prominently from his close-cropped, scrub brush hair. There was a sweat stain in the middle of the undershirt. Someone said something in a very loud voice and Danny's father's back convulsed with spasms of laughter.

Hours of time somehow disappeared as the light crept through the panes and it was morning. Maybe that first morning, maybe not. Birds were noisily coming alive in the dark trees. From far out on the lake, he heard the buzz of an outboard motor, and the unmistakable smell of frying bacon came to his nostrils from an adjacent cottage. Danny slipped out of his bed and tiptoed, his bare feet cold on the hard floor, to the other side of the open loft. He gently shook his mother to tell her the good news that morning had arrived. But it was all in vain. Some inscrutable adult logic postponed the start of the day. Three times he was sent back to his bed, with its sagging mattress and strange mold-scented comforter, until the birds and motorboat and bacon pushed him to insanity again and forced him to plead his case once more to the lifeless mounds in his parents' bed.

But eventually he was to see the water lapping listlessly at the narrow, sandy beach and the green-painted rowboats bumping against the oil-drum pontoons that supported the wooden pier. And he heard the shouts of children and the hoarse barking of dogs. As the blazing sun rose, he frequently stopped to look out over the water, appalled by its strangeness. It was now like a tepid soup, and tiny bugs, illuminated by the sun, were abuzz over its surface, seemingly of no interest to the fish slumbering in the mud and weeds below. Danny had not yet learned to swim and so was forbidden near the water. An unnecessary warning because he was still terrified of its murky uncertainty. His father spent much of that afternoon in a hammock strung between the cottage and a catalpa tree, snoozing off what Danny later supposed was a substantial hangover.

But that nap, to Danny, years later, had its poignant shading. "Why do you sleep, Daddy?" Danny thought, "when you have so short a time to live." He was glad that his father, feeling better in the coolness of late afternoon, rose and got his tackle and went out to the end of the pier. There, apparently pleased to be by himself for awhile, he cast, Danny thought rather expertly, trying to hook one of the bass lingering in the lily pads. Danny went out to be with him and his father turned and looked at him and smiled, saying nothing. Again and again, he cocked his wrist and sent the lure soaring in the yellow sky, toward the lily pads. His thumb carefully adjusting the flow of the line as it hissed off the reel.

The long afternoon became evening. The expanse of meadow behind the cottage, where Queen Anne's lace had stood listlessly in the fetid heat, unmoved by even a tiny breeze, turned first orange, then blue. Eventually fireflies arrived in such numbers that their blinking iridescence lit the meadow the way Michigan Avenue had been decorated for Christmas before the war. Danny's father continued to stand quietly in the dusk, his arm and hands rhythmically repeating the motion of the cast, his face impassive. Certainly he was unaware of two pairs of eyes watching his every move with great intensity. Two eyes very close at hand, filled with admiration for his strength. Two more studying him from a very distant future, trying to perceive his weakness.

He felt a nibble, tried to set the hook, and there was a languid splash near the lily pads as a bass eluded the lure. He cursed once, very softly under his breath. Shortly, with a barely audible sigh, he reeled in the line for the last time. Then he carefully repacked the tackle box, with the lure in its designated compartment, the reel wrapped in a chamois bag. He kept the rod together to be leaned against the wall in the kitchen for the next day's fishing. Then he headed up to the cottage with Danny tagging behind, trying to walk in his father's shadow created by the lantern that hung on the end of the porch.

That August slid by in endlessly long days. He played every day with the Johnson boys, getting underfoot at the public dock which smelled of the outboard motor brew of oil and gasoline and faintly of the buckets of minnows, swimming in tea-colored water, and wooden boxes where redworms crawled in black humus. He drank lemonade under the catalpa trees and fought noisily with the other boys for turns lying in the hammock. Afternoons, he often swam off the dock in the warm water, safe in his mother's arms and buoyed by water wings. On weekends, he rode in the boat far out and around the lake with his father and Mr. Johnson.

The war seemed very far away for everyone, though the men had to return to work during the week, because every plant was running three shifts and every hand was needed. But, without a newspaper arriving on the doorstep each morning and no electricity to power a radio, it was hard to believe there was anything special about those times. The women and children continued their easy routines through the long hot days. There were wet swim suits to hang up, sandwiches to make, and errands to run.

Still, Danny knew about the war. At the cottage, he kept a magazine in a hidden drawer in the loft, with pictures of soldiers dying on distant beaches and wounded men staring out of red-soaked bandages. The pictures both terrified and thrilled him and he returned often to the drawer to peek once more at the images of carnage. Though the falling bombs were a world away, violence visited in the form of angry summer storms. Great black clouds rolled in from the south. Then suddenly a chill wind sent newspapers and sand buckets tumbling across the yard, ripped towels off the clothesline and made the boats bang hard on the pier. Then the rain came down in sheets and hammered on the roof. The now-gray surface of the lake boiled with raindrops. One had to shout to be heard above the torrents. And the cold breeze rummaged through every nook and cranny of the house. He and the Johnson boys huddled in the attic in delicious fear, watching the rain streak and run on the panes.

Then there was Danny's dream, which first occurred when he was a young man back in Chicago and revisited once in awhile ever since. Sometimes there were new variations. When he felt the dream begin, he became alert in a strange way, even though he was sound asleep, anxious to see what else might be revealed this time.

In the dream, he was his father. Returning home from the lake on Sunday night. Tired, sunburned, a little hungover. The city was very hot, fatigued with the prolonged August heat. When he opened the front door, a blast of it met him. But he was not tuned particularly to any sensations at this point. He threw his gear down, not caring that some of it completely missed the chair near the door and the casting rod, disassembled neatly in three pieces and wrapped in canvas, clattered on the floor. He found himself on the steps to the basement. The air was much cooler down there. He walked slowly down the rickety steps.

As his eyes adjusted to the light, he could see things in the basement, things that gave him pain to look at. The washing tubs and ironing board and curtain stretcher and other paraphernalia his wife used to do the family wash. His son's tricycle and his daughter's old baby buggy. His workbench, with tools and scrap wood in a clutter. In all of this disorder he finally found what he was looking for. A length of strong manila rope. He put an apple box in the middle of the room, below a length of pipe that ran along the ceiling. He got up unsteadily on top of the box.

Danny always awoke wide-eyed and shaken from the dream, wondering at the kind of immortality his father had managed to achieve. What else could a common man do to make his presence felt across more than half a century? To phrase a riddle so cleverly that the search for its answer would always seem a worthwhile obsession. And that was exactly what it was, Danny realized, pure obsession. As he grew older, he realized he probably never would know the exact reason for the suicide. He had learned that life seldom serves up the tight, little morals one finds in novels and movies.

What Danny finally figured out was that all of this was really about him. The abstract images of a father he could barely remember never would have driven him to such compulsion. But, in the act of dying, this seemingly simple man had created something very significant, a doubt. A doubt so terrible that it colored almost everything Danny ever did. His father had cracked under x amount of pressure. What was his break point? How much could he stand?

Danny realized that his own strong survival instincts had much to do with the fact his father had been unable to survive whatever had tormented him. Was it possible, he sometimes wondered, that he carried this historic failure like an anti-body against his own occasional despair? This was not a very comforting notion to him because it seemed to reveal his motives as no better than anyone else's he knew. Across all that time and space, wasn't he . . . he asked himself . . . just trying to compete with his old man?

The Girl on the Bus

I never really intended to leave Loraine. But one night I found myself on the back stair, bag in hand, obviously going somewhere. It really wasn't all that spontaneous. I had spent hours, pacing back and forth in her apartment, allowing the tension to grow, filling my head with the idea of not seeing her ever again. Figuring just how much that hurt. But all this simulation seemed to balance just fine with the idea of not putting up with her crap for one more minute. Then there was the business of hauling all my accumulated junk down the old stairway. Boxes and books and loose clothes. Up and down the stairs. There was a deadline for all this. Loraine was supposed to be home at eight, had confirmed that around six, with me saying "okay" as if I weren't thinking what I was thinking.

There was this final tense moment when I hesitated, then slipped my key under the door and that was that. I ran down the steps, the first stage of my flight, as though Loraine were chasing after me, brandishing her big, Williams-Sonoma chef's knife. At the corner, I stopped the car and looked back at her building which seemed to rise up like a tramp steamer in the murky night, seemed to have its own soul, an exasperated, all-suffering Loraine soul. I allowed a tug of conscience for her at that point, seeing her reading the note I had left in the middle of the living room floor. So, my first tears were actually for her.

For the first half hour or so, my mind still toyed with the option of racing back to intercept Loraine, to wait for her at the door and snatch up the key and note before she could. To sneak my stuff back into the apartment later. But I drove on, up the Coast to L.A., the moment for retreat approaching and passing. And then up through the cold, dark Central Valley, with the lights of its isolated towns blinking listlessly on the horizon. Bakersfield, Visalia, Fresno and Merced emerged and receded in the night.

Well, I thought, grasping in my mind for anything positive, this is America. This freedom to escape, balanced with this need to escape. So American to be on the road, to move from gas pump to diner, to eat enormous, greasy breakfasts of sausage and runny eggs and biscuits. The pulling back onto the highway like a coming home to Mama. The lights cutting through the tule fog as the all-night talk show host drones on.

Where do I go from here, I wondered. Already I was sick of being alone. I struck up conversations with waitresses. I considered stopping at a phone booth to call into the talk show. I thought about Loraine. I thought about Stephie, whose house in Santa Rosa I was heading toward, though I hadn't quite confirmed that with myself. Loraine couldn't seek comfort like that. I don't know many women who could. But a man could. I could take my hurt inside Stephie's body and feel good for awhile. I could cry into her, my tears running on her naked breasts. But there was something else in me that didn't want that either. What I really wanted, I decided, was to find the girl on the bus. The one I saw on the California Street Morning Express one morning five years before, with the meadow of pink skin behind her ear, that scant piece of Heaven between her corn silk hair and the collar of her coat. That's what I wanted. A gleaming future made entirely of materials not presently at hand.

All of this hope and energy (I couldn't sleep if my life depended on it) were locked within the bubble of my Toyota. I was transported through the night as though that movement was my reason for being. The terrible pain in my stomach, the loss of Loraine, I happily knew was temporary. And when the light began to appear over the blue mountains to the east, I realized I had made the only decision I could have. That's a wonderful, soaring feeling. I knew quite well that night would someday take its place in the comfortable, running narrative of my life, a thing that carries no real weight other than its movement from the one thing to the other.

ALEXANDER
THE GREAT

My old friend Judge Stone used to say you can only do so much in one lifetime. When I think back on it, about the only thing I ever did that anyone would care to hear about was that I knew Alex Mobley personally. If you know much about the game of golf you probably find that pretty interesting. Alex was, in the opinion of many people, the greatest golfer who ever lived. He also pulled some pretty weird stunts along the way, like blowing a nine-stroke lead in the U.S. Open and walking away from a great professional golf career in handcuffs. Most folks think of golf as a pretty clean show, where you never see the dope and criminal stuff that goes on in other sports. But Alex Mobley was just the kind of guy who could change a thing like that.

Now I know a lot of people can't say much good about him. I can understand that, but I'd just as soon not hear it said to my face by some stranger. Everybody in West Blairsdale feels the same way. After all, this is the town where our local weekly *The Bugle* called him "Alexander The Great." At Shady Hills, where Alex and I both played, we just called him "The

Kid," and said it with a lot of respect. Funny thing too. Later on, we also got to calling him "The Man." How many heroes you ever heard of who made that jump?

Maybe none of this is gonna make any sense if I don't tell you a little bit about our town. West Blairsdale is the kind of place where the day you're born you know you got one strike against you. Kind of dirty and ramshackle, it sits in bottom land in the bend of a muddy little trickle called Chipmunk Creek. One big factory is left, a box fabrication plant, and it's on hard times. There's a couple of machine shops that'll fold when the box factory closes and a mean little downtown with streetcar tracks running through the old bricks on Main Street, even though there's been no streetcar here in forty years. Grass grows through the cracks in the streets and curbs and all the letters to *The Bugle* don't seem to change that. On Main Street, we got two bars (The Pharaoh and Ned's) and Miller's Pool Hall to take care of our recreation.

That's about it except for the golf course which you can't miss if you're driving on Road 57 through town. You just take a left at the end of Main, and for awhile you'll still be paralleling the railroad tracks and a bunch of vacant lots with high weeds. Then you'll pass the American Legion baseball park and the high school where Alex went. About where the speed zone ends and Road 57 runs on to Stanton, there on your left is Shady Hills Golf Club.

I hope you're not expecting Augusta National 'cause brother it sure isn't. Picture a beat-up white clapboard building with a big red Coca Cola sign. That's the pro shop and clubhouse. Inside, it smells like somebody peed on the floor and there's three or four card tables set up in the clubhouse side, always filled with the usual assholes, slapping down the cards on the table in gin games, the way you hate to see men play. In a little room off to the side, there's a snack bar and a Blennd machine with a clear plastic top so you can see that yellow stuff swirling around in it. A bunch of hot dogs are always spinning around in the infrared oven, whether anybody's around to eat them or not. Some of 'em look like they were around when Truman was President.

But compared to the course, the clubhouse looks pretty damned good. Talk about a miserable golf layout. I don't even know where they got the Shady Hills bit. There're no trees to make shade and most of it's flat as a pool table. The fairways are all dry and pockmarked, especially in August when the sun bakes that course into a damned desert. Now, on a two-bit layout like that, it doesn't take much to get on the greens, 'cause all the holes are pretty short and the ground's so hard, the ball'll roll forever. But once you do get on, you sure better have a steady hand on that putter. Those babies are like a Teflon skillet and the ball bounces all over the place. Every year, the "Greens Committee," which is what we call that bunch of drunks that has the most to say about everything, debates whether the club should just give up and put in sand greens. But like most subjects around Shady Hills, we just can't come to a decision.

Does that sound like playing at Shady Hills is no fun? Don't believe that for a second. Maybe playing golf there has been the best time of my life, even better than being in the Navy in Hawaii. A lot of that, I guess, was those no-good bastards I teed it up with eight months of the year and played cards with the other four, for more years than I can count. A hell of a lot of faces have come and gone in all those years, but there are some I guess you'd call the real regulars.

Of course there was Red who used to own the place. Until Red died nobody knew he was the owner, because he always said he was working it for someone else. We all figured there was so much bitching about the sorry state of the greens and the crapper in the clubhouse and everything else, it was just easier for him to shrug and say that was because his boss was such a sonofabitch. And then of course, there was Red's daughter Ruthie, who was the sweetest, most good-natured, moon-faced little gal you'd ever wanna meet. About the only thing bad you could say about Ruthie was that she always had the hot pants and there was not a taker in sight. I mean if anyone was willing to overlook Ruthie's looks, they sure didn't want to step a round with Old Red.

Then there were the players. Just about all of us had nicknames, and none of them seemed to fit all that much it seems to me. First of all there was Sparrow, this scrawny redneck who never talked and nobody had ever seen where he lived. Someone said he lived in a truck body in the weeds behind Fowler's Garage. I don't know about that. I do know he worked as a night watchman at the box factory so he'd have his days free for golf and fishing. I don't think he really looked like a sparrow. More like a snake or something, the way he moved his head kind of loose and crazy when he walked. As a golfer, I don't know what to say about him. Sometimes you'd look at those sorry-ass clubs of his and that funny swing and you'd let him slip up on you and win the hole. But not that often.

Judge Stone was another guy who could fool you.

Always talking about some bullshit, yack yack, yack, and first thing you knew you'd miss a putt listening to his crap. Of course that's what he wanted you to do. And if you ever saw him swing . . . you know, he had that kind of fat man's cut where he couldn't even finish up the shot and had a little curly-cue follow through where he looks like he's holding up a flag or something. For that matter, he was no judge. Kind of a two-bit lawyer who mostly sold a little real estate.

And there was Fizz O'Connor, big old red-faced drunk. And his name didn't fit either, though I guess the Fizz must have had something to do with all the boozin' he did. But Fizz drank nothing but Early Times with tap water and that sure don't fizz. See what I mean about the nicknames? None of 'em work. But that's like Shady Hills being flat and having no trees. And for that matter, why West Blairsdale? There wasn't an East Blairsdale or even a plain Blairsdale. Sometimes, when I think of stuff like that, I get a headache.

Who've I left out? Well, maybe Gimme Phillips, who was this colored guy we always played with. The Judge once said, when all those country clubs on the PGA tour were being forced to let blacks in, that maybe we were way ahead of our time. Well, let's face it, when you lived in West Blairsdale and played at Shady Hills, it was a little hard to put on airs. Gimme was an okay guy. Strung up a little tight, maybe. But he could hit that ball pretty good even if he couldn't putt a lick. As for the Gimme bit, that's a little hard to figure. I guess just one time he asked somebody for a gimme on a tricky four-footer and got stuck with that nickname for life. We play rough at Shady Hills.

And finally, Dirty Floyd, who was just like his nickname. Rough, hard-drinking sonofabitch and a pretty good golfer, even though he was missing some fingers from a punch press in the box factory. Until The Kid came along, he was the perennial club champion and was usually in the money at all the crazy tournaments we had through the year. I gradually got to liking Old Dirty, but never thought he was anything but white trash. If there was some hill-ape way to look or act, you could bet he'd find it every time.

Now about The Kid. Alex. Everybody's got a story about when he first came around Shady Hills. But I don't know that he was all that unusual, especially when he was young. He was just one of those nice kids you run into once in awhile. Always had a big smile and was real polite to all the men. He grew up in a raggedy-ass trailer park a mile or so away with his mom. I don't think Alex ever knew his father and nobody here remembers him much except for what a bastard he was. But I knew his momma well enough to know she probably put her hand up the side of Alex's head a time of two to make sure he stayed the way he was.

So, he was just hanging around for the first few years, asking Red if he could run the mower and looking for lost balls in the ragweed along the highway. Wearing this big old Ben Hogan kind of cap somebody gave him that was too big for him then and hung down over his eyes. Later on, Red started using him in the clubhouse, selling Blennds and hot dogs and cleaning up a little (as much cleaning as there ever was in that place). We kidded him a lot so you know we liked him. But you just couldn't hurt that boy's feelings or get him sore.

I don't know to this day if Red was the one who first put a club in his hands. All I know is one day I saw him for the first time hitting some balls out back of the clubhouse. Shady Hills didn't have a practice range, but sometimes, if you felt like you couldn't live without hitting a couple, you could go out there and knock some down the line between the maintenance shed and the highway. You could either hit some clunkers with smiles in 'em and forget about 'em. Or go pick 'em up. Well, one summer evening I saw The Kid out there, hitting balls, and it was like I wanted to rub my eyes and look again.

Now I know how to part a man from a sawbuck on a Nassau, but that's mostly a head kind of thing. The truth is I got a swing, like most of us at Shady Hills, that comes in about five pieces and looks as ugly as old people fucking. But I do know what real golf looks like, and I could tell right off that this kid had the stuff. He stood up to the ball like he really knew what he was doing. And when he swung, he sure didn't look like the rest of us, trying to get back to the ball like there was a fire or something. He had a nice, smooth swing and he was mashing that ball pretty hard, even then.

In the next few years after that, he began to grow. First he got tall, then he filled out real broad in the shoulders. Not many guys would be kicking this boy's ass, we could tell that. And man was he a pretty-boy. Anytime you were with him, you could see the women around acting kind of strange. I mean from these little high-school girls on up to waitresses my age. But he didn't seem to let all that attention get to his head too much. He was still The Kid.

"I seen the little shit with some cute gal over by the school," said Dirty Floyd. "She was looking at him like she'd do it for him right there on the street.." We were all having a cold one one Spring afternoon at the Pharaoh, that dumpy bar I told you about down on Main.

"Oh my," said the Judge, shaking his sunburned bald head, "to be young again like that." He took a big pull out of his Bud with his eyes raised to Heaven like he was dreaming.

"Like that?" chimes in Gimme Phillip's, "there never was a day you were like that kid. You sure as hell couldn't hit the ball like he does. And I don't see some little split-tail doing you in the street." We had to agree with Gimme. There was something about that kid that made you envy him even back then.

Then Fizz said something that I still think about 'til this day. "I wonder what his mother thinks," he said. "Watching that boy growing up and guessing what's gonna come out in the end, a sweet soul like herself or an asshole like her old man." They all shook their heads, thinking about that.

"Well now, listen here," I said. "That boy's got a perfect right to be whatever he wants. He doesn't have to be either one." I sure as hell meant it too.

There are athletes and there are athletes. But, I think Alex would have been one of those great ones no matter what he'd done. He played a little baseball, and he could put a few over deep center, which at the American Legion Park, is a mean poke 'cause they built that outfield fence real high so people wouldn't be spraying balls all over Henry Street. And when he was only a sophomore, he was the starting fullback on the football team. Fizz and the Judge and I went over to the school one Friday night and saw him playing against Lemmity Consolidated, and we all said he looked like a man among boys out there. Those Lemmity kids never did stop him, even though it was a damned hot night in early September and I think Alex was a little pooped and wasn't putting out on every play. So no telling what he could've really done.

But all that didn't last very long. Alex was hooked on golf just like he had been when he was a little boy. I can understand that. It's a damned good game for people who know how to play it. And man, did he know. He could turn that big tall frame real slow and easy on the ball, and I mean flat crush it. Now, we all never thought of Shady Hills as a real layout and knew it was pretty easy. But Alex made a joke out of it. Short as those holes were and as hard as the ground got, he was in range of every one of them off the tee. That even included the Seventh, a kind of double dogleg that passed for a par five. When Alex was feeling a little daring, which you have to be because Chipmunk Creek comes into play on the right side with a lot of sycamores lining it (the only serious trees on our course), he just cut across the doglegs, creek and all, and went for the flag. Made it sometimes too, on a damned par five.

The amazing thing was he was just as handy around the greens. Alex, I suspect, already spent more time at Miller's pool hall than his momma knew about. And he appeared to be one of those guys who really understands pool tables and golf greens. A putter in those big hands was just as dangerous as his driver, and he could sure make that ball behave on those horrible greens of ours.

The Kid still carried around an old wedge Fizz had given him. By now he could practically play tunes on it. When Shady Hills burned out every year, which seldom was any later than June, most of us just left the wedges in the bag and rolled everything around the course. But The Kid had that hand action like the pros do. He could practically hit that wedge off the cart path and make it stop, and so help me, even back up on the greens.

So golf was his game now. Boy was the football coach sore when he found out the best fullback he ever had wasn't suiting up anymore. Gimme noticed one day that The Kid always showed up at the course, coming from the south, instead of along Maple Street which ran straight to his trailer park. Alex acted a little sheepish about it, but Gimme kept on pressing, and finally he admitted he didn't want to walk past the high school field, cause the team was practicing and they gave him a lot of crap when he passed by. Big Red wasn't all that happy about the way things were going either. By now, The Kid had found he could make so much money winning bets from suckers like me and The Judge that he didn't see much point in selling hot dogs and sweeping floors anymore. So Red lost his assistant.

Oh could that Kid hustle. I mean, there was no way any of us could handle him, but like damned fools, we kept making bets with him. What a sight we must have been out on the course. I mean you got a foursome with some goofy looking guy like Sparrow and a bunch of numb-nuts like Fizz or Gimme or the Judge or me. And here's this big strong kid, striding along with us down the fairway and swinging that club like a damned pro. I mean, he'd give us all at least a stroke a hole and sometimes more. Or we'd play best ball against him. Or we'd make him play us with just a wedge and a putter. But still, his very worst game was better than our best.

There was one ugly time in there when The Kid holed out a half-wedge on Dirty Floyd and took the smirk right off his face. Floyd was sitting up there on the green with his ball a foot from a sure par, and The Kid shoves an eagle at him, which even with the stroke he'd given Floyd, takes the hole. I thought for a minute Dirty was gonna have a piece of him. He's standing by the ball-washer on the next tee, watching The Kid putting his wedge back in the bag, and you could see how red his face was and there's a big vein popped out across his forehead. There was a time when Floyd hit the shots that took all our money, but that day apparently was over. So I can't say I wanted to be in The Kid's shoes that minute. "Listen, you little shit," Floyd said, "you wipe that smirk off your face 'fore I do it for you. Just 'cause you beat me, don't mean you can act like that."

That was sure turning into some bad scene at that point, but The Kid looked up at him in a way I figured was gonna make everything all right. "Gee Floyd," he said, his face all puzzled-looking, "I wasn't smirking at you. You had a nice approach on that hole. I was just smiling 'cause of how lucky I was on my pitch. The Judge and I kind of stole a look at each other. That was a nice piece of diplomacy, we thought. The kid probably saved himself an ass-kicking, though you never know about that, 'cause, as I said, he was a good-sized boy. But he gave Floyd back a little bit of his pride, and he didn't even have to back down and act cowardly doing it. Dirty himself shook his head at the skill of it. I think he realized he had not only been out-golfed, but out-bullshitted. So, he went over and shook Alex's hand and everything was all right. After that, nobody ever went to bat more for The Kid than Dirty Floyd.

By then, Alex was starting to gain some fame outside Shady Hills. Red suggested he take a crack at the State Junior. So The Kid packed up his beat-up old bag and second-hand golf shoes and hitch-hiked down to Hamilton where they were having it. And damned if he doesn't come in second. Now, that was amazing when you think about it because he'd never played on a real golf course. And somebody was kind enough to show him how to hit a sand shot, 'cause he never had before. And they had a lot of trees there which was something else new. But nobody at the State Junior had ever seen a boy smash drives like The Kid. Or do the things with the wedge and putter like he could.

So there he is in the newspapers, not just *The Bugle,* but *The Clairmont Times* and even *The Hamilton Journal.* The Kid brings a whole handful of newspapers back and we all read 'em in the clubhouse and said "golly gee shit!" and "can you believe this?" Even way back then, the sports writers liked that angle about Alex as the regular guy's champion. That thing Snead and Trevino and Arnold Palmer had. They wrote all about his second-hand shoes and his mismatched clubs and how he stuck it to those snot-nosed country clubbers. Of course we all ate that shit up with a spoon.

But there was this Mr. Fairbanks over at Big Oak Country Club near Cedar who thought Alex should have a little more going for him than what he had at Shady Hills. So, he cooked up this assistant-to-the-pro job and offers it to Alex. If The Kid would help out a little around the pro shop, he'd see that he got some lessons and a chance to play regular on a real course, I mean with lush, green grass and sand traps and trees and everything. Well hell, Alex jumped all over that, even though it meant Fizz had to loan him his broken-down old Chevy pickup to drive the twenty miles over there every day. Right away, we all missed having The Kid around all the time, but everybody was real happy he was getting a chance.

Well, things changed pretty fast after that. I think by the time the State Junior came around the next year, Alex didn't even bother to play in it. He had already won The District and the State Amateur. Can you believe that? They said at the time The State Amateur win was a fluke. There was this great player, Norb Updike, some big car dealer who had won the Amateur and The State Open several times. In the final match, he had some trouble with the intense July heat, they said, and he got into some trouble on the sixteenth and so on and so on. "Fluke huh?" said the Judge. "We've all seen that fluke shit before. Alex started leaning on that driver on him, right?"

"And rolling in the side-hillers," Gimme added.

"That's right," said Sparrow, and we all looked at him quickly 'cause that was only about the second thing Sparrow had said that entire year.

Well, Alex may have seemed like a country boy to the big-shots of the game, but we never saw him like that. When he came around to Shady Hills back then, which he did surprisingly often, he really classed-up the joint. He wore these good looking lamb's wool sweaters and nicely-pressed golf pants, and he had two-toned white and alligator golf shoes. And the clubs, Goddamn it! Nobody ever played a round at Shady Hills with clubs like that. I can remember one evening, just before dusk, Alex went out and tossed a bucket of balls down on the first tee and we all gathered 'round to see what he was gonna do. So, he gave us a little exhibition, and it was the damndest show I had ever seen, except on TV maybe, but here it was right at Shady Hills. And he's hitting off that nasty scuffed up tee box such shots as would make you cry. Big soaring iron shots that he'd learned from the pro at Big Oak. And drives so long they were scary. Fact is, on that first par-four hole, short as it was and the fairway baked hard, all his drives were going past the green When he was done, and we all applauded like we'd just been to the circus, Big Red said, "that was nice, Alex, but who's gonna pick up all those balls?" And The Kid turns to him, with a big smile across his face, and says, "those are all brand-new Titleists, Red. If you pick 'em up, they're yours." A nice deal, I thought, 'cause there sure wasn't gonna be a scratch on 'em the way Alex hit the ball. Red could sell 'em to the suckers for two bucks apiece.

Yeah, The Kid would still play a round with us once in awhile. But things were different now. He'd leave the bag and just carry a couple of irons and a putter, cause he really didn't need a wood. And he'd flat carve our little course apart, like a real touring pro would, which left us feeling kind of funny. I don't know quite how to explain it except that it was humiliating in one sense that this was our course he was doing it to, but some pride too that we even knew a player of Alex's ability and had watched him grow up. For sure, he wouldn't take our money anymore. Not a single bet. But he'd tell us about some big scores he had made on those rich members at Big Oak, and he sure didn't need Fizz's pickup any more, cause all that easy money got him an almost new Mercedes that sat in the lot behind our clubhouse.

I still kind of marvel at The Kid's loyalty to the old home town. I mean, by now, he could go anywhere and write his own ticket. But still he'd come around and see us, and can't really say why. I remember the first time I ever saw his Sondra was in the Pharaoh, for God's sake, which if I didn't make my point before, was some real low-down dive. I mean it was dark as a tomb and you could smell the urinal the minute you walked in. If you dropped anything less than a five-dollar bill on the floor, you'd probably let the sonofabitch lay there. It was that filthy. But still, like a lot of dives like that, we'd keep showing up every couple of nights. Fizz and The Judge and Gimme and me. Dirty practically lived there. We always went there when Gimme was with us 'cause at Ned's, Old Ned himself didn't like having a black guy in his place and gave Gimme dirty looks and served his burger on waxed paper instead of a plate like the rest of us.

This night, all of a sudden, Alex walks in with this real fancy woman. Well, we all turned and looked with our eyes bugging out. I should tell you that The Kid was only about eighteen or nineteen then, and it's true he only got into our town bars because he had fake I.D. and because he was Alex. Everybody in town knew he wasn't twenty-one, even though among strangers he could pass for it. He even had this dark beard you could see real plain even after he shaved. But this gal, she was at least twenty-five, maybe a few turns past that. And damn, was she a sight. "Boys," Alex said, "this is Sondra. Sweetie, this is the greatest bunch of guys you ever met." And he introduced us all around and we nodded our heads and acted stupid.

Now, I know that Sondra never thought we were the

greatest bunch of guys she ever met. But she sure was up to the game, which on her part I think, was some first class slumming. Alex pulled out an empty chair for her and she sat down, and we could smell her perfume real good. Like I said, it was dark in The Pharaoh, but even half blind, you could see she was flat gorgeous. Long black hair pulled back, her forehead high and glisteny. And she had that kind of long, sleek body that makes fellas say something like "the closer to the bone, the sweeter the meat."

"Sondra's a member at the club," Alex told us, a big grin on his face. "I'm giving her some lessons."

"And what are you giving our Alex," Floyd asked her, looking her right in the eye. As I told you, Dirty never forgot for a minute he was trash.

She didn't flinch but took time to accept the cigarette The Kid had offered her. He lit it for her and she slowly let out the smoke.

"I'm giving him some lessons, too," she said in a husky voice.

Of course, we all hooted and carried on and I guess in the next hour fell totally in love with her. But I remember thinking, I hope The Kid knows what he's doing with a grown-up nut-cutter like her. I guessed right then this boy wasn't going to stop for a minute 'til he had everything this world has to give.

I'll share one more story from that particular time. I think it was November. Certainly it was well into the winter, and though we managed to play pretty much year 'round, even when it got real cold, I don't think anybody was out on the course at the time. We were all bunched up in that old clubhouse and had the place so full of smoke you could hard-ly breathe. Red didn't like boozin' in there, so we were kind of sneaking a couple of bottles around in the paper bags, and the cards were slappin' on the tables. In the middle of it all was The Kid. Sitting at one of the tables in one of his expen-sive sweaters and leaning back against the wall while he played. Among other things, he'd become a pretty good card player. So there was one more way he had to take people's money and have 'em eating out of his hand. If I recall, I think the week's pay Sparrow had originally set out in front of him was almost gone.

Well, Red and Ruthie were both there, but Red was busy fixing the counter in the pro shop where he kept the balls and merchandise he sold, running an electric drill and ham-mering something and cussin' a little from time to time. But Ruthie was hanging around, leaning on the little swinging door of the snack bar, listening to the conversation. It was real obvious to everybody that she was into The Kid like she had gone completely crazy. You know what I mean. She had this silly grin and her plump body was kind of moving around almost like she was dancing in place. So we all started doing a little kidding. "What're you kids doing hanging around us old men?" I remember Gimme asking.

"Hey, that's right," Dirty Floyd muttered, looking up from his hand. Floyd looked to be pretty much loaded, even though it was only early afternoon. "You two could be rootin' around out in the maintenance shed."

"Now Floyd," The Judge said, "you shouldn't talk that way to these nice kids. Shame on you."

"Judge, you telling me The Kid doesn't know what

rootin's all about?" Dirty shoots back. "And just look at Ruthie here. She'd love to have this boy in her pants. Wouldn't you sweetie?" Of course we all moaned and wheezed at that.

"Come on Dirty," Alex said, as easy and relaxed as he could be. He was long past being rattled by anybody even though he wasn't much out of high school. "Of course I'd be honored to be with Miss Ruthie here. And with a nice girl like her, I'd be on my very best behavior." More hoots and squeals from us bunch of assholes. Of course, the big joke to us was the idea of Alex, who ran around with the likes of women like that Sondra, would even bother to unzip for Ruthie. But of course, he was, as usual, doing his charming thing by saying he'd be honored.

Who knows why Ruthie hung around putting up with us. Maybe she was just used to our talk. But I suspect she thought it was worth it on the slimmest chance that maybe, with enough sparks flying around, something might catch fire. Time to time, her eyes would flick to The Kid, and there was no doubt what her wildest dreams would be. "I tell you one thing, Dirty," says Fizz, "If her daddy hears you talking like that about Ruthie, he'll nail you up to this wall here."

Dirty took a drag off his Lucky and discarded a couple of cards with a big slap. It became obvious, to me, that a lot of this yacking he was doing was for covering up how much he liked his hand. I decided to fold. "Shit, I ain't afraid of Red," he said, finally. "Besides he's making too much racket in there to hear us."

"Tell me kid," Gimme chimed in, "if you was to get together with Ruthie, where would you go? Maintenance shed, or in that nice car, or what? "

"I think in the pro shop, Gimme," Dirty Floyd said. "That'd be about perfect. Break her over the counter like a shotgun and pop her from behind. That sound right to you, Kid?" We all hooted again, and Ruthie felt obliged to say "now you cut that out, Floyd." But she was smiling.

Of course, The Kid had to say the right thing for the moment. Or maybe he was covering a hot hand, too. "For Ruthie," he said, "I'd say nothing but the best. Maybe that new Holiday Inn near Stanton. Honeymoon suite." He looked right at her with a big smile. Damn was that Kid smooth. And Ruthie's got her moon-eyes locked right on him. If you didn't know better, you'd have thought it really was gonna happen.

Then suddenly the room is full of Red. "Listen, you dickheads, how much of this shit you think I'm gonna take?" he roars. The room goes dead silent. Red's bald head is glistening with sweat and he's puffed up like he's either gonna kick every ass in the joint or drop dead with a heart attack, one or the other. He was one fierce sonofabitch, I gotta admit. No one dared to put a card down 'til he was finished. Then he turned right at The Kid. "And what gives you the right to come in here and think you can talk like that to my daughter? You think you're so damned special you can act like that right in my own place?"

Boy, there it was, right out in the open. We could all see in a second that maybe something had been chafing Old Red for a long time. Having this kid come in and take over like he had since he was practically a boy. Too good to sweep up and sell hot dogs, he was out hustling us yokels on the course when he's still knee-high to a flagstaff. And now, in his pretty sweaters and all his money, he's hanging around insulting Red's daughter. We were all pretty nervous at that minute, mostly scared that The Kid would huff out and never come back. Fizz even started to say, "Aw, he didn't mean . . .," but he shut up. We were all waiting expectantly to hear what Alex would say. It was like that day when Dirty was going to take on The Kid when he lost that hole. But a lot of time had gone by since then, and the balance of power had shifted. I think if The Kid had said something like, "Oh, fuck off, Red," he might have led us in a mutiny. What the hell, Red needed our business. And were we gonna let him insult The Kid?"

But then Alex spoke. "God, Red, I'm sorry. You're right. I've got no call talking like that in your place. And as good as you've been to me, that's flat not right. Will you accept my apology?" Well, of course, Red finally sputters that sure he will and no hard feelings. There's so much emotion in that room, it was a good thing that only Ruthie let it show as the tears rolled down her cheeks. Of course, as the card games and the yacking resumed, The Kid had moved up still another notch with us.

It wasn't long after that day that Alex wandered on. Mr. Fairbanks at Big Oak helped get him a golf scholarship at the University of Houston, although he didn't last there very long. For awhile, he was the assistant pro at the country club, and of course, he was winning every tournament around the state. The newspapers were full of his exploits, and every time you turned around, there he was, smiling out at you from the sports page with some trophy in his hand. That's when Jay Erner at *The Bugle* started calling him Alexander the Great, which I always thought was a cornball kind of nickname anyway.

In fact, it was right about then, that Alex got his real nickname changed. I remember it very clearly. We were all sitting around at Ned's, most of us that is except Gimme, which was probably why we were there. Anyway, there was some kind of sports show on the TV over the bar, and suddenly there's a clip of Alex rolling in a ten-footer to win the State Amateur for the umpteenth time. The Judge just kind of sighs and says, "well, there's The Man doing it again. Just like he'd take me for ten bucks on a press." Strange how something like that'll happen. Almost from that moment on, we all started calling him The Man. Except, of course, on those rare occasions he showed up at Shady Hills where we still called him The Kid to his face.

Those were busy times for Alex. We all had assumed he would be a big touring pro some day, but it was nice to see it begin to happen. He went to the PGA school and then Mr. Fairbanks found him some sponsors for his first year on the tour. Then, there we were, sweating out that year, tournament by tournament, as he tried to break in. It was hard to imagine someone as talented as he seemed to us being just one of the boys. The tour was full of guys who could lay a three-iron on a dime at two-hundred yards.

But still, Red got a dish on the roof and bought the big cable package just so we could see as many tournaments as possible. Only once in awhile would we catch a glimpse of The Kid walking down the fairway with his threesome. A lot of times, he didn't even make the second-day cut. We were all starting to get a little nervous.

He traveled alone that first year, and Fizz had a cousin

over in Columbus who told him The Kid was certainly doing it in style. Pretty much a big party every night and never at a loss for a good-looking babe. But that part was bound to change too. One afternoon around the holidays, when the tour was done for the year, all the assholes were hanging around Shady Hills wasting time, when the door banged open and in, out of the cold, walked Alex and Sondra. Oh, could that woman fill a room. We were all struck dumb and fumbling around trying to shake hands and offer her a chair and everything. Ruthie got kinda swept out of the room as though somebody had done it with a broom. Alex and Sondra were both dressed to the teeth. The Man was wearing a suit that'd probably been a year's pay for me. And that woman was flat gleaming. Damned was she a looker.

She's also wearing a big flower on her dress, and we soon find out that they'd been married that very day. I can't imagine how he talked her into seein' us on an occasion like that, but there they were and she was smiling just as big as him, if you can believe it. We all kind of thought they'd get hitched sooner or later, but in a big church wedding with some big damned spread at the club. But, Alex told us, since this was her second, she didn't want to do that. So they just went to a justice of the peace, and there they were, big as life, at Shady Hills. Red was so surprised, he let us take our bottles out of the sacks and pass 'em around freely. That Sondra could drink right out of the bottle like a man.

When Alex started his second year on the tour, she went with him. I don't exactly know if that was the way he wanted it, but there she was anyway. Maybe that put a stop to some of the cocking and boozing, which probably helped his play a bit. Of course, he was just a little smarter and more experienced too. He seemed to do things a little different, like clubbing down for tight fairways and paying attention to the openings to the green instead of blasting away recklessly with his driver. But, whatever it was, his fortunes began to improve. He made the cut more often than not, and sometimes he finished up in the money, pretty close to covering his expenses I guess. We saw him a lot more on TV and we'd scream and holler and carry on every time he out-drove somebody. Sometimes, the commentators acted like they knew who he was, and they'd say something about how long he was off the tee or what a good putter he was. And we'd all puff up like Christmas turkeys and look at each other and nod our heads.

And finally it happened late that year. Alex won the Kemper Open, coming out of nowhere on the last day. It all worked out so that he was on a hot streak on the final five holes while the leaders were all taking the gas. So he never did have a lot of pressure on him and won by a couple of strokes as it turned out. By then, the TV guys had the book on him. Big, big hitter, they said. Great touch around the greens. Grew up in a trailer park in a small town. Hustled for nickels at a little nine-holer (nickels my ass, I thought. The Kid never took anything from me that made a clinking sound). Overcame all the odds, they said. I don't know that I went along with all that Abe Lincoln crap. Seemed to me like Alex had it made from the beginning, but I guess it's how you look at it.

Well, can you imagine how we took this? We had all been at Shady Hills, watching the tournament, and of course there was no tension, 'cause we didn't know 'til practically the seventeenth that he was gonna win it. But when he holed out that final putt, the room exploded. Everybody hollering at once and hugging and banging each other on the back. You couldn't hear yourself think.

Old Red was afraid he'd quickly lose a celebration like that to The Pharaoh. So, he broke his rule in a big way and had Ruthie pick up about six cases of beer and a bunch of food, and we had the biggest party that day I ever saw thrown in West Blairsville. Such whooping and hollering as you never saw. I don't think anyone played a single hand of cards or even sat down around the tables. We were all too busy getting drunk and loud. And right in the middle of things, here shows up this Western Union messenger all the way from West Fork with a telegram. Red opened it, his hands trembling while we all quieted down a bit to have him read it to us. THIS ONE'S FOR YOU BOYS. ALEX.

Didn't forget his pals, we said. There's nobody like The Man, we said. Jay Erner, the sports guy from *The Bugle* even showed up now that he knew Shady Hills was gonna be some kind of shrine like Abe's Cabin or something. I suspect he may have thought better about coming over when he saw the party going on. At one point, I saw Dirty Floyd get him in a headlock, bellowing drunken shit in his face. "Fuck that Alexander The Great crap, asshole! Call him 'The Man' like his buddies do!"

"And we are his Goddamned buddies, too!" This came from nobody else but Sparrow. We all yanked our heads around to see that drunken redneck grinning like a fool. Boy, everybody took a piece home from that day.

Late in the evening, The Judge and I went outside to take a piss. That stinking toilet in the clubhouse couldn't keep up with us that night, and everybody'd been pissing off the little rise that went down to the first tee. So we're standing out there in that nice cold air, with our heads spinning from all the beer and excitement. "Well, I gotta tell you something," he said, "it's just possible this is the best day of my whole life."

"Me too," I admitted.

"You know, I've lived in this two-bit town all my life," he said. "And it always seemed like the real world, the world where things happen, you know, had nothing to do with me. It was like another planet."

"I know," I said.

"Well," says The Judge, "right now I feel like I'm in the real world. Like maybe what I am and the place I live in amounts to something. Jesus Christ, if I live to be a hundred, I'll never forget this."

Well, the fun wasn't over. After the tour broke up for the year, Alex came by a few times and told us he had some big plans for the next year. Having Sondra along had made a difference and he was really focused, he said. It started out looking like that was the case. He was in the decent money almost every tournament. He was a close second at the AT&T and won the Bob Hope Classic fairly handily. As a tournament winner, he got invited to The Masters and nobody could fault him if he was a little overwhelmed with all that Southern rich-boy shit and didn't make the cut. He was still on a roll. Then along came June and the U.S. Open at Pebble Beach.

We had all talked about how we were all going out to California for the Open, but of course, nobody managed to pull it off. It was worse that the day before the show started, Alex called us from Monterey and said he had really been hittin' the ball and thought he could make a real run for it. "That's it," says Fizz, "let's get in my van and go there."

"Damn, Fizz," Gimme said, shaking his woolly gray head. "That's over two-thousand miles. Time we get there, it'll be over. "

"Well, we gotta be there for The Man," he says.

"Maybe we can send a bunch of telegrams," I suggested, "but it looks like it's gonna be the old TV set for us."

Well, it got more painful that we weren't there as the next few days unfolded. As usual, some unknown had the first day's lead, but Alex was up there with the leaders. We got to see him, in a replay, holing out a chip. On the second day, he took the lead by two strokes. And on the third, he played in the opinion of the announcer, "one of the great rounds we have ever seen here at Pebble Beach." That usual furious ocean wind died down a lot, the sun was out, and the sky was the deepest blue you ever saw. Old Alex let it all out. The crowd oooh and ahhed all the way around as he kept bashing drives past everything. He wasn't clubbing down that day. Even on the tight holes, out came that driver and he flat went for it, over the traps and doglegs and everything. At the end of the third day, he had a six stroke lead.

Being the Open, they had those greens skinned and rolled 'til they were like concrete. "Just like Shady Hills," Alex had said on one of his calls. "All you gotta do is touch the ball and it's got a mind of its own. I just imagine I'm out there, taking a Nassau from The Judge and Sparrow.

"Goddamn," Dirty Floyd said, licking his chops, "The

Man's got 'em this time."

"I think he's finally coming of age," Gimme said.

There was a lot of tension the evening before the final round. We were going over to The Pharaoh, but somehow we didn't and wound up hanging around the clubhouse. A couple of gin games got started, but nobody seemed to care about it. "Well hell," said Red, "it's only seven o'clock out there. Let's give him a call and wish him luck. We'll all get on the phone."

"Good idea," I said. But when we got his room, Sondra was there by herself.

"I can't tell you for sure," she said, "but I think he gave me the slip." She wasn't nasty to us or anything, but you could tell she was a little pissed.

"Hmm," said Fizz, when we had hung up, "them old habits die hard, don't they?"

None of that seemed to make any difference as the next day started. When Alex teed off in the leader's foursome, his six-stroke lead was still intact and it looked like he was off on another tear. "I'm not coasting on it," he had said in an interview before the round that they ran while he was walking down the first fairway. "Bold got me here. And that's the way I'm playing today."

Well, the way he was playing that didn't seem like reckless talk. The wind stayed down again so he could do what he wanted. And what he wanted was to bring that tough old course to its knees. The Man was going drive-wedge-putt, drive-wedge-putt on some of the classic holes in the game. He got an eagle and two birdies before he hit the turn and had added three more strokes to his lead. Nine up with eleven to go. Are you kidding? They could start writing the check.

And you should have seen him on TV. He looked like a movie star, walking up that fairway, grinning and waving to the crowd. Boy did those galleries love him. He was what golf was to each of them. A game where you don't pussy-foot. Where you go for it. So, nobody was prepared for the 8th. You know that par four with the carry on the second shot over this big inlet in Carmel Bay.

Alex lagged a 3-iron off the tee and was in the garden spot to put the ball on, comfortably short of the inlet and about 165 yards from the flag. He pulled out a 8-iron, which we all remarked wouldn't have been enough club for your average touring pro. Then he stepped up there real confident and . . . God I don't know what. It was an awful shot, some kind of crazy duck hook that didn't come close to clearing the water and clattered down among the boulders. Well, he looked at his 8-iron like it was broken or something, like it had nothing to do with him. He turned and smiled at the gallery, a real smile, not a cover-up. I don't think he felt the least bit panicked. There had just been this little mistake, and what's a one-stroke water hazard penalty when you've got a nine-stroke lead? "Stick it on the fuckin' flag, Kid!" Dirty was on his feet, red-faced, yelling at the TV set.

"Shake it off, Kid," Gimme said, still leaning back in his chair against the wall, with no lapse in his confidence. "Just get home. You got 'em."

Well, The Man looked pretty comfortable setting up to the next shot. But there must have been some gremlin in the mechanism somehow, 'cause he does the opposite of the first shot, like his body is playing games with him. Instead of coming over, he doesn't come enough, and the shot, unfinished, starts drifting right on him a little. Anywhere else but the Open, he might have caught a piece of the green or at least been up for any easy chip. But, of course, they've got all the apron either skinned or grown up with tall rough, whichever will cause the most trouble in any one place. So Alex's shot catches a little skinned-off spot and kind of takes a bad bounce right and then rolls back a little toward the inlet. There's a gasp that goes up from the gallery like maybe he's gonna put another one in the drink. The ball does hold up, but it's in some untended ground near the edge of the cliff.

Well, we all catch our breath while Alex's threesome walks around the inlet. If you looked at The Man walking beside Barney Carlisle and Scott Henry, the second and third lowest scorers in the tournament, you'd have trouble figuring who had done what. Alex was joking with the gallery about what a damned duffer he was, like everything was hunky-dory. Barney and Scott are walking along, heads down, like it's the end of the world. But actually they're just puzzled at what was happening. Until then, they must have pretty much accepted the drubbing they were taking and mostly thinking about which one of them was gonna get the second money. Then, all of a sudden, there's an opening for the title itself. Both had hit good shots to the green and Barney even had a good run at a bird. And no telling what was gonna happen to Alex, who already was lying four and still thirty yards from the hole. "Go get 'em Kid," we kept yelling at the TV.

When they get to the other side of the inlet, The Kid walks all around the ball and confers with an official. For Alex, he looks pretty damn worried. "Piece of fuckin' cake!" Dirty hollers. "Just like Shady Hills, Kid."

"That's right, Kid," adds Fizz, "it's your routine Shady Hills lie." We all laugh, caught up in the idea of it. Sure as hell, Barney and Scott never saw as many shitty lies as Alex had.

But this was no two-buck skin game Alex was in. I'm sure as he kept looking over the shot and practicing his swing, he was thinking, this is the stuff that makes heroes. I come up stiff to the pin from this shit in the U.S. Open, who's gonna forget my name? He'd never have some sniveling choke thoughts in his head. Still, the announcer, whispering with great drama, pointed out that The Kid had sweat on his forehead even though it's nice and cool out along that cliff. I noticed that myself in the close-ups and couldn't help but thinking about Sondra saying he had "given her the slip." To do what? To fuck some bimbo 'til the sun came up? To drink up all the whiskey in Monterey?

It's hard to say whether the lie was just too tough or there was a little choke gas in The Kid too. But he sure didn't hit it stiff to the flag. The shot came away clean all right, and maybe if he had played it a little safer and gone for the fat of the green, he might have been all right. "Bold got me here," he had said on that interview. So now he's only twenty feet from the stick, but he's in that nice tall Open rough with a downhill chip on to that slick green. Alex made sure he got enough of it to get out clean, but the ball just wouldn't stop 'til it was in the tall rough on the other side. Well, I'll spare all the details of that nightmare, though none of us were spared that afternoon. When it was over, Barney did have his birdie and Alex carded a big fat nine. Six strokes of the lead gone in the blink of an eye.

Well, there isn't much more drama to lay on here in my

story. Barney Carlisle is suddenly all puffed up like Popeye in one of those cartoons after he eats the spinach. He knows he's gonna win it. And The Kid, well, The Kid has totally taken the gas. The smile he has on his face is so weak we can see not even he believes anymore. The sweat is not only standing out on his face, but is even soaking through his light blue sweater. "Goddamn it, he choked!" Dirty Floyd screamed in anguish. "The Kid choked!"

It was all too true. There were no more nines. But now, he was stumbling from one bogey to another, while Barney turned the jets on and started really playing championship golf. On Pebble's famous eighteenth, he holed out a birdie putt to beat The Kid by three full strokes. Can you believe it? And Scott slipped in to beat him out of second by a stroke. By then, nobody at Shady Hills could even speak. We sat numbly, staring at the screen, taking our punishment like Alex had.

Well, who the hell could guess Alex blowing the Open was just the beginning of his woes? The next week, he was playing an exhibition in Peoria, before hopping the plane to the British Open. At that point, the people at the club who had paid big money to have him probably wanted it back. Of course some folks would come just to see what kind of guy would fuck up a finish that bad. Maybe he could demonstrate that duck-hooked 8-iron that had made him famous. Anyway, we all knew he was in Peoria and didn't think much about it. But the next morning we wake up. and there in a big headline in *The Bugle* is ALEX ARRESTED ON DOPE CHARGE.

I guess I've learned to expect almost anything out of life, but that one just left me gasping. Without another thought, I drove over to Shady Hills where a crowd was already gathering, even though it had been raining so hard nobody was gonna be playing any golf. I went right up to The Judge who looked like his wife had just died.

"What the hell happened?" I asked.

"They got him with some cocaine in his car," he said.

"Why the hell would he do a dumb thing like that?" I asked.

"Fizz got a call through to him this morning. He's out on bail, but it doesn't look too good. The Kid says he was all fucked up 'cause Sondra left him two days ago. Says he doesn't even know how the dope got in his car."

"Let me get this straight, Fizz," Gimme suddenly says, joining the conversation. "That woman left him, just 'cause he blew the Open?"

"No shit?" Suddenly Dirty Floyd's with us too. "What kind of cunt would do that? Leave a man 'cause he doesn't win the biggest tournament in the world? Jesus Christ!"

"Well, we don't know that for certain," I said. "And we're just getting The Kid's side."

"Well, I'll take the word of The Kid over that bitch, anytime," Dirty shoots back.

"Me too," says Gimme. Well right off, some things had changed. Everybody had seemed to like Sondra okay until she left The Kid. Now, she was dirt. And the other thing was, I began to notice how everybody had drifted back to calling Alex "The Kid" instead of the "The Man" since the Open. Everybody seemed to have something to say about it all except Sparrow. Not talking was perfectly normal, but for some reason he had this strange sheepish expression on his face.

Fizz managed to get a hold of Alex in Peoria and told him he should come down and see us. I don't even know to this day if that was in the terms of his bail. But damned if he didn't come. That afternoon, there he was, sitting in the clubhouse, takin' a nip out of the old bottle and playing cards. Sure as hell, he didn't have any problem talking about what had been happening to him.

Shot for shot, we got the whole story of the Open, which didn't sound anything like what I thought I saw with my own two eyes. First of all, he bragged about the first three days and half of the fourth like a man who'd won it. What great shots he'd hit, what the gallery said to him. I don't ever remember Alex braggin' like that. One thing I'd always liked about him was the way he let his talents do the talking. Then, he got into the shots at the 8th. He never said shit about choking and he seemed so intense nobody had the nerve to suggest it or even ask him a question about it. He said he was trying to fine-tune that 8-iron to the green a little too much. He was gonna put some backspin on it so he could back it up to the hole off the high collar of the green. A little too much fine-tuning that he duck hooked it into the gorge? Kind of hard to believe I thought. On that pitch that wound up in the deep greenside rough, he said his lie was so bad that he had a terrific argument with that official about whether he could move it. All that ground had been torn up with maintenance equipment, and the ball was down in a scar the machine had made. And so on. The bogies finishing up were all caused by similar calamities. He felt like he'd been screwed out of the Open title.

As for Sondra, he could see this coming a long way off. Never should have let her go on the tour with him, he said. She was always butting in his business. Every time he wanted to go someplace, she had to know where he was going and what he was doing. And she was always asking him questions about money. Just because she knew how much he made in each tournament and how much he got for endorsements, didn't mean she knew about all the money he made. A guy like him had lots of ways of making it. And it wasn't any of her business as long as he brought home the dough, which he sure as hell had been doing. Through all of Alex's story, the clubhouse was pretty quiet, even though every chair was taken and some of the boys were standing up along the wall. A few, like Floyd and Gimme, threw in some encouraging words from time to time. But Fizz and The Judge and me and most of the others were just quiet. None of us were all that big in this world, but we had done a little business. When you're in business, you get to know bullshit real well when you hear it.

Well, nobody had to wait long to see how the wind really blew. One Friday morning in August, *The Bugle* ran a headline so big it took over the whole front page so you had to turn to page two to start reading about it. ALEX MOBLEY ARRESTED AS GANGSTER.

Well maybe they got a little carried away. The Kid was hardly in the company of Capone or Luciano, but he was in deep shit trouble for sure. The charges were dealing in narcotics and what they called racketeering. The federal narcotics people had raided his house in Cedar, which was near the Big Oak Country Club. Sure enough they found cocaine again, but this time it was in bundles, all ready for street sale.

They also found a lot of stuff that properly should have been in other folks' houses. It turns out, as the story unfolded, that Alex had set up a kind of gang, right here in the sticks. There was a little action with baseball and football cards, but mostly it was selling dope and breaking in houses and fencing the goods. It was pretty well organized and there were a lot of people mixed up in it. Even when he went on tour, Alex had found he could still run the business long distance.

So, as it turned out, Alex had been up to something for a long time. Almost from the time he was winning the tournaments around here and being the assistant pro at Big Oak. I kept thinking about how disgusted Big Red had been when The Kid was in his early teens and got too big to help Red around the clubhouse. I think it always was like that with Alex. Wherever he went, he made friends real fast, with all kinds of people too, from bank presidents down to the lowest kinds of trash. And wherever he went, there always was an easy way for him to make money. People admired The Kid a lot. I guess we always imagine a gang boss as some hard-ass. It's like everything else; some guys get there on charm.

It took me a long time to wrap my poor old dumb head around such a strange story as that, putting all those sorry facts up alongside the picture I keep in my head of The Kid's face. Even today, though years have gone by to soften things up, I get to thinking about Alex and the way he could play golf, and for a minute I'll forget about all the rest. It's like the way it was when my Thelma died and I'd sometimes think something good about her and forget that she wasn't around any more.

Life went on at Shady Hills pretty much as usual. The

only difference was that The Kid wasn't there to talk about and worry over. Oh yeah, and Sparrow wasn't there either. He turned out to be the only one of us caught up in the gang, at least the only one who got caught. Sparrow was part of the house-breaking end of the business. The rest of us went on with our golf and fishing and knocking back beers. The Judge and Red both died in the same year which kind of cut a hole in things for awhile. Ruthie ran the business pretty much like Red had, and we all kept bitchin' about the greens and everything else. Ruthie didn't take that shit to heart, not even as much as her old man had. A good-hearted gal.

And oh yes, there was one more thing. Years after Alex had served his time and moved away to God knows where, Fizz and Dirty and Gimme and I drove up to Chicago one Saturday to see a Cubs game. Coming back that night, we stopped to get some supper at a restaurant off the interstate. Kind of a fancy place for the likes of us, but we were damned hungry and didn't care. Well, who do you think is sitting in there in the bar? Sondra. A little older and harder looking, I'd say, but still a pretty good-looking babe. She's sitting with some guy who was at least as old as me, but a hell of a lot richer-looking.

I was glad to see her and we said some howdy-dos when we came in. But you know Dirty. He just had to do his trash act. After we put down a bunch of beers, to go with all the ones we had at the ball game and polished off some steaks and were fixing to leave, he takes it in his mind to go up and say something to her. We were almost out of the place and suddenly he's standing by her table, his face all red. And I heard him say something to her about how she led Alex into trouble and then ducked out on him when he needed her.

Well, just like the first time we met her, Sondra had that sense of timing. She didn't say anything for a second or two, then she looks all of us up and down as we're standing there. "You know who ruined Alex?" she finally says. "You sons of bitches did." And she turns away from us so cold that even Dirty gave up and walked away from her without a word.

We didn't talk much about what Sondra said on the way home. It was late and Floyd and Gimme were soon sawing logs in the back seat while I kept up a steady chatter about anything I could think of to keep Fizz from falling asleep at the wheel. We sure never mentioned it again from that night on. People still do talk about The Kid and now we laugh about him a little and tell jokes about what happened, I think because that's the way we all get by in this world. I know, as long as I can still swing a golf club, bad as I do it, and lift a cold one with my buddies, that's what I'm gonna do. I've seen some hard times like anybody, but most of my days are filled up with the things I like. I just can't see much sense in worrying about what might have been.